The time had come

A drop of perspiration rolled over the bridge of Nile Barrabas's nose, dangled from the tip, then fell and smashed itself against the corner of his right boot.

Barrabas didn't notice. A sound from the jungle drew his attention, and still immobile, he let his eyes probe the greenery. It was like a living wall, a wall that slowly started to shift with a faint but growing chorus of rustlings.

Barrabas was ready to act, to signal the others. When the patrol came into view, he sighted along the M-16, then squeezed off a single shot.

C000038089

SOLDIERS OF BARRABAS

THE BARRABAS EDGE

JACK HILD

A GOLD EAGLE BOOK FROM
WORLDWIDE®

TORONTO · NEW YORK · LONDON · PARIS
AMSTERDAM · STOCKHOLM · HAMBURG
ATHENS · MILAN · TOKYO · SYDNEY

First edition September 1988

ISBN 0-373-61626-0

Special thanks and acknowledgment to
Joe Roberts for his contribution to this work.

1

President Manuel Colon relaxed in the back seat of his limousine, going over the speech he was to deliver in his mind. His adviser, General Caesar Trieste, had arranged the occasion so he could address students at the university and impress on them the importance of a good education. Colon laughed to himself. It was all publicity. He himself had never gone to college, and found himself called upon to explain to college students how important education was.

Colon hated being a hypocrite, but he had to admit that Trieste's idea was politically sound—and being a politician often had one walking a fine line between truth and hypocrisy.

Colon noticed then that his limo was slowing and he leaned forward to check the reason with the chauffeur. "What is the problem?" he asked.

The man did not answer. The limo slowed even more, then pulled off the road and finally stopped.

Colon knocked loudly on the glass partition to get the chauffeur's attention and shouted, "What is wrong?"

At first he thought the man had not heard him again, but then the partition began to slide down. He waited until the glass had lowered completely before repeating his question. "What is the trouble, driver?"

The driver turned and, smiling, said, "No trouble, *presidente.*"

"Then what—" Colon started, but he stopped when he saw the gun in the man's hand. He frowned and opened his mouth to protest. The driver took that opportunity to fire into his open mouth. The bullet tore out the back of the president's head and smeared it all over the rear window.

The driver opened his door, stepped out, opened the back door, pressed the barrel of the gun against Colon's right temple and fired again. This time it was the left rear window that became splattered with blood.

The driver slid the gun into the shoulder holster beneath his left arm, straightened his jacket and calmly started to walk away from the car.

SIX MEN APPROACHED the home of Julia Berbick, the sister of the vice president of El Salvador. The leader sent three of them around to the back and then approached the front door. When he was satisfied that he had given the others enough time to get to the back, he lifted his foot and slammed it against the door just above the doorknob. Wood splintered and the door flew open.

The three men entered the house with their guns drawn. A pretty girl of about fourteen came down the hall to see what the commotion was. She had straight black hair and a sweet mouth that was now cast downward. When she saw the men her lovely brown eyes widened, but before she could say anything, one of the men shot her between her budding breasts.

They swept through the house quickly. They found the vice president's sister in the kitchen, and before she had a chance to react did the same thing to her that they had done to her daughter.

One man went upstairs and found a twelve-year-old boy in his room, reading a comic book. Before the boy could lower the comic, the man fired right through it. The comic jerked with the impact, and the bullet struck the boy between his upper lip and his nose, killing him instantly.

When the man returned downstairs, the leader said, "Well?"

"He was not upstairs."

"He is not down here," the other man said.

The leader looked at both of them and said, "He was supposed to be here!"

The other two looked helplessly at their leader, who chewed his bottom lip. He was going to have to explain this to Generalissimo Trieste—no, to Presidente Trieste—and he was not looking forward to it.

NILE BARRABAS LOOKED OUT the window of his Orlando hotel. From there he could see one of Orlando's tourist attractions, Church Street Station, a collection of small gift shops and theme restaurants that had been built within an old railroad station. He had landed at Orlando Airport only two hours earlier, having come to Florida at the behest—and insistence—of Walker Jessup.

Barrabas had been in Switzerland with Erika Dykstra, enjoying some leisure time after the SOBs had gone through a particularly harrowing mission in Thailand.

As he always did when he woke in the morning next to Erika, the white-haired man sat smoking a cigarette, watching her sleep. Oddly enough, the statuesque blonde had become over the years more friend than lover. Barrabas supposed that everyone needed one true friend in his life, and for him it had become Erika.

At that point the telephone had rung in their suite. He had unplugged the bedroom phone, and so he rose and walked into the living room to answer it.

There was only one person the caller could be, because only one person knew where he was.

"Hello, Jessup," he said immediately upon answering.

Walker Jessup was not amused, or impressed. "The Fixer," as he was known in some Washington circles, had other things on his mind.

"Nile, I need you in Florida."

"Florida?" Barrabas said in surprise. "Why Florida?"

"I'll tell you when you get there."

"Which will be when?"

"Tomorrow."

Barrabas had looked through the door of the next room and saw Erika lying on her stomach on the bed, but looking over her shoulder at him.

"All right," he said.

"Go to the Sheraton in Orlando and wait for me. I'll contact you tomorrow."

Before Barrabas could say anything, Jessup had hung up. The big mercenary replaced the receiver and sauntered back into the bedroom. Erika was resting her chin in her hands, staring at the headboard.

"I have to go to Florida," he said.

"I know."

"I have to leave today."

"If there's a flight."

"If I know the Fixer, there's not only a flight, but a reservation."

"Of course."

"Where would you—"

"I'll just stay here," she said. She switched her position so that she was lying with her cheek on the back of her hands. She still was not looking at him, and in fact did not look at him even when he was leaving.

It had become an all too familiar ritual to her, and at last, the understanding between them went beyond demands, and beyond words.

Now Barrabas was in Orlando, where he had found a reservation waiting for him at the Sheraton. Though he wasn't in downtown Orlando, he was close enough so that he could see downtown Orlando. In what was supposedly one of the fastest growing cities in Florida—along with St. Petersburg and Tampa—Nile Barrabas did not see all that much to be impressed with.

There were several high buildings, which invariably turned out to be banks, and skeletons of others still going up, and of course there was a jai alai fronton and two dog tracks, but the city had suffered a blow by losing its USFL football franchise. Currently the city fathers were fighting with St. Pete and Tampa over the possibility of a major league baseball franchise. He had also heard someone say in the hotel lobby that Orlando would soon have a thoroughbred racetrack—something that Tampa already could boast of. And, of course, there was Disney World, but that didn't do much for the actual physical growth of the city except fill the hotels with tourists.

Once Orlando had done its growing, perhaps then he'd return and see what the city was like. Right then he had no desire to go out and see it and only wanted to hear why Walker Jessup had needed him to fly there so quickly.

He was lighting a cigarette and considering ordering lunch from room service when the phone rang. This time he didn't assume that it was Jessup.

"Yes?"

It was Jessup. "Can you see Church Street Station from your hotel window?"

"Yes."

"Meet me at Apple Annie's in twenty minutes."

"Apple Annie's?" Barrabas repeated, not sure he had heard correctly.

"Apple Annie's," Jessup said and hung up.

Well, Barrabas thought on his way out of the hotel a short while later, maybe he'd get lunch out of it.

But he was disappointed all around. Up close, Church Street Station—which was on West Church Street, just east of Interstate 4—was depressing. Of course, it did not actually come alive until evening, and this was noontime. The place was deserted, except for some diehard tourists who were going into the shops.

Apple Annie's was directly across the street from the Cheyenne Saloon and Opera House, and right next to Rosie O'Grady's Good Time Emporium. Both of those establishments served lunch. Apple Annie's did not. It was a sort of garden that served frothy-looking drinks of many different varieties, most of them containing fruit.

Barrabas hated drinks that contained fruit.

He found Walker Jessup seated at one of the white wrought-iron tables with a concoction of some sort in front of him. It was frosted, and white, and was in an Apple Annie's glass. Only three other tables were occupied, all by families of varying sizes, and all far enough away so as not to pose the threat of being over-heard.

"They tell me this is some sort of a fruit daiquiri," Jessup said as Barrabas sat down. Barrabas was surprised that the wrought-iron chair the Fixer was seated in was holding up under his considerable bulk. "They also tell me that I can take this glass home with me."

"Why are we not having lunch?"

"I'm trying to cut down."

Barrabas snorted, and then spotted the gravy stain on the lapel of Jessup's suit. The man had already had lunch without him. Considerate of him.

"Why the urgent summons, Jessup?"

"Urgent matters require urgent summonses, don't you think?"

"You going poetic on me?" the big merc asked.

A waitress came over and seemed to find Barrabas's white hair and firm, jutting jaw irresistible.

"Can I get you anything?" she asked hopefully. She had to be three whole years out of high school.

"Bring whatever he's drinking," Barrabas said.

"Yes, sir. Right away."

"Take your time," the warrior said.

She rushed off, and he knew that she wouldn't.

Jessup leered at him. "How's it feel to have that effect on little girls?"

Barrabas shrugged. "It's either that, or I scare them. You want to talk to me?"

"Central America."

"If that's what I came all this way to hear—"

"We have a problem in El Salvador."

"What kind of problem?"

"Our man there has been overthrown."

"Your man being..."

"The former president," Jessup said, "President Manuel Colon."

"And he's been ousted by..."

"New President Caesar Armande Trieste."

"And you want to get Colon back into power?"

"That'd be pretty damn difficult," Jessup said. "They say Trieste has Colon's head on a pike behind the presidential palace."

"Why not in front?"

"Maybe he doesn't want to scare the neighbors."

"Okay, so you're screwed in El Salvador."

"We can't leave Trieste in power," Jessup said. "He's very receptive to advances from the Russians."

"Tell me what you want, Jessup."

"We want him out of the way," Jessup said.

"And what else?"

"Colon had a vice president named Berbick, Jules Berbick. We want him put into power."

"Is he also 'your man'?"

"He will be," Jessup said. "There's one problem with that, also."

"Which is?"

"He doesn't want to be president."

"You sure know how to pick 'em, don't you?"

"I don't do the picking, Nile," Jessup said, "except where you're concerned."

Actually, Jessup didn't pick them. There was a House committee that did the picking, and Jessup in turn contacted Barrabas and his SOBs. The SOBs were a covert action team that operated under the strictest secrecy. If they were ever caught, they could expect no help from the United States government.

Still, they accepted the missions they were given, and they followed Barrabas faithfully. They were rewarded with money, but that was not their primary concern. They wouldn't do just any job. Their sense of right had to be involved. And beyond that they reveled in the knowledge that they had cheated death once again and come out on top.

They were all misfits who needed the rush they got from the action that was involved in their line of business. It was the only profession any of them knew, and the only one that would ever accept them.

"If he doesn't want to be president, why is he cooperating?"

"Trieste's men killed his sister and her two kids, a twelve-year-old boy and a fourteen-year-old girl. They had also expected to find Berbick there—he lived with them—but he had been called away unexpectedly."

"Uh-huh," Barrabas said. "Would you like to spell this out to me clearly?"

"I want you to go in, find Jules Berbick and his followers, train them, take Trieste out of office and put Berbick in."

"Just like that?" Barrabas said. "What about this training business?"

"Berbick has some men with him."

"Am I to be dealing with the Contras, the rebels, here?"

"Uh, no," Jessup said, looking uncomfortable. "You see, the Contras weren't very happy with Colon, either. As far as they're concerned, there's not much difference between Colon and Trieste."

Barrabas waited for more, and when it didn't come, he said, "So what do you consider 'some men'?"

"Berbick's got about fifty or so."

"Against the Salvadoran army?"

"Think about what you're saying," Jessup said wryly.

"I know what I'm saying," Barrabas said. "If Trieste's men are Soviet trained, then they're good."

"As good as you and and your people?"

"Don't try flattery on me, Jessup," Barrabas said testily. "It doesn't sound natural coming from you. How many men does Trieste have in his militia?"

"We don't know."

"So I'll have fifty, and I don't know how many Soviet-trained men I'm going against?"

"We're still trying to find out the full strength of the Salvado—"

"Yeah, all right," Barrabas said.

The waitress appeared then with his drink. She smiled and seemed to perform a kind of curtsy as she tried to set it in front of him. So intent was she on studying his face that she almost set it down on his lap, but he took hold of her wrist and guided it to a safe landing.

"Thank you," he said.

"Anytime."

He waited until she'd drifted out of earshot, then resumed his questioning. "How are Trieste's men armed?"

"Soviet AK-74's."

"And Berbick's men?"

Jessup fidgeted in his seat. "You'll arm them."

"With what?" Barrabas asked sharply.

"With whatever you can buy," Jessup said. "This is to be an independent mercenary operation, Nile. Even more than usual we can't be connected with it in any way."

"And what do I do for money?"

"There's an envelope in the hotel safe—which *you* had put there when you registered."

Barrabas leaned forward and asked, "Is there enough money in the envelope?"

"You'll have to make do."

Barrabas leaned back and reached for the drink before he came to his senses. He didn't touch the glass but stared at Jessup with hard eyes. "This is all on the qt, isn't it? Where'd the money come from, petty cash?"

"We have to be careful these days, Nile," Jessup said. "The Contras hearings, and Reagan's bill just being turned down—"

"I don't want to hear the politics of it, Jessup," Barrabas said, holding up his hands.

He thought it over. Going against Soviet-trained and -armed troops with inexperienced men who were probably going to be cheaply armed and barely trained . . . it *was* an interesting proposition.

"Do we know where Berbick is?"

"In the mountains. We have someone who can lead you there. You'll do it?"

"Was there ever any doubt?"

"No."

"We'll need some men to carry the supplies once we land."

"I'll see to it. You'll be going by water, naturally. Where will you be leaving from?"

"It'd be easier if we were leaving from Mexico. Why'd you drag me down here?"

"This is where our intelligence is coming from."

"Well, don't you worry about where we'll be leaving from," Barrabas said. "All I'll need from you are coordinates for landing. When I need them, I'll let you know where I want to land."

"Yes, but—"

"I thought you didn't want to be connected with this?"

"We don't."

"All right, then. I'll need Hayes, Nanos, Billy Two and Lee Hatton. You already are aware that Nate Beck won't be in on this one, and Bishop is off on a private errand."

"I'll find the others. What about O'Toole?"

"I know where to find him. Oh, don't tell them anything you don't have to."

"I always leave that to you."

"Let me know as soon as possible if you've gotten hold of them, preferably by tonight."

"Right."

Barrabas stood to leave.

"Uh, there's one more thing you should know." The Fixer looked sheepish.

"What's that?"

"Trieste's got a, oh, a death squad, for want of a better word. People who oppose him suddenly turn up missing, or dead. His coup was almost bloodless, because he left it to this squad. They killed Colon, then drove Berbick into hiding, and Trieste took over."

"What are you telling me?"

"That all you might need to do is eliminate this squad of his, and the rest might fold like a house of cards."

"Well," Barrabas said, "that would be convenient."

"I'll leave a message about our next meeting," Jessup said. "We'll continue to use the hotel safe as a drop."

He turned to leave.

"Are you going to drink that?" Jessup asked, indicating Barrabas's drink.

"Hell, no. You can have it."

The waitress saw Barrabas leaving and her shoulders slumped. Her friend, who had been the recipient of some whispered confidences, patted her on the back consolingly.

Jessup looked at Barrabas's drink, then looked at his and shuddered. He remembered that the place across the street was called the Cheyenne Saloon and Opera House.

BARRABAS WALKED BACK to his hotel, and by the time he reached it, he was drenched. Rivulets of sweat ran down between his shoulder blades, and his shirt was hopelessly crushed looking. The clothes he was wearing he had brought with him from Switzerland, and yet it was only June in Florida, just prior to the really hot summer season.

Before returning to his room, he stopped at the front desk.

"Yes, sir, can I help you?" the clerk asked. It was the same young woman who had checked him in. She was about twenty-five, slender and pretty. Although he usually wasn't bothered by gawking women, he was relieved that she showed no great interest in him other than wanting to be helpful.

"I'd like to retrieve that envelope I put in your safe when I arrived, please."

"Of course, sir. Your name?"

He gave her the name he had checked in under, and she got the envelope from the safe and handed it to him.

"Are you enjoying your stay?" she asked with genuine interest.

"Immensely."

She smiled at him and then went to answer a ringing telephone.

Up in his room he opened the envelope and found some money inside. He counted it, then dropped the envelope on the writing desk. It was enough—if he were outfitting a Boy Scout troop.

He undressed and showered. When he got out of the shower and toweled off, he found a full-length mirror behind the door. Absentmindedly he paused to study a body that had undergone years of both discipline and misuse. He was six foot two of hard muscle and scar tissue, and he hadn't been kidding when he'd told Jessup that women were either fascinated by him or frightened. Some women looked at the scars on his body and didn't care, women like Erika Dykstra and Anna Kulikowski. Other women felt some unnamed fear or were even repelled by the scars.

He shrugged, left the bathroom naked, put on a T-shirt and shorts and dialed a number in New York City.

2

Alex Nanos tore up his tickets and flipped them into the air, watching them flutter to the floor. He was muttering something darkly, and a scowl shadowed his face.

"You must like doing that," Billy Starfoot said to his friend. "You do it after every race."

The Greek gave the big Osage a sour look.

"You won, huh?" he asked.

"Of course," Billy Two said. "The gods were with me once again."

"You've been playing dogs with Indian names!" Nanos said incredulously. He was hoping that Billy Two was not going off on one of those "Hawk Spirit" tangents that he'd been prone to since he'd undergone some heavy treatment at the hands of the GRU. Actually, Alex had been finding the big Indian's behavior almost normal and had been relieved by it.

"Not just Indian names," Billy Two said. He pointed to the program listing for the third race, the race just run, and to the name of the winning dog.

"Osage Chief!" Nanos said in disgust. "My dog had a better record . . . and a better name."

"I know," Billy Two said. "Old Greek Joe." The big Indian's tone was tinged with glee.

Quickly Nanos looked at the listing for the fourth race and gave a satisfied grunt. "At least there's no dog in this race with an Indian name."

"Or a Greek one," Billy Two pointed out.

"Now I'll show you how to pick a winner!"

"Not just now," Billy said. Nanos looked at him questioningly, and Billy inclined his head. Nanos looked in the direction of the nod.

Liam O'Toole stood talking to another man, and his racing program was stuck into the left-hand pocket of his jacket.

That was the signal that he had made contact.

"Bingo," Nanos said.

THE FIRST MAN TO ARRIVE in Orlando had been Liam O'Toole. After talking to Barrabas on the phone, he had caught the very next flight out of Kennedy, and had been met by the colonel at Orlando Airport that night.

They had dinner in a restaurant on International Drive called The Olive Garden, and Barrabas outlined the mission to him.

When he was finished, O'Toole asked without hesitation, "What about the others?"

"Alex and Billy Two will be arriving in the morning, and Claude and Lee Hatton at least by tomorrow night. You've got to get to work today. We need weapons and a boat, and we haven't got much money."

"That means you want me to use my Irish charm."

"I want you to use whatever you have to," Barrabas had said, then added, "even that."

It had taken O'Toole a full week of sifting through contacts, old and new, before he finally made the appointment at the Sanford–Orlando Kennel Club, to meet his man during a Friday night racing card. Nanos and Billy Two were sent in to back him up. All three were sporting the loud shirts that most tourists affected when they visited Florida.

The contact was Cuban, that much was obvious to O'Toole as the man approached him. O'Toole was to have one program in his right back pocket, and another in his left-hand jacket pocket. Once the contact was made, he had arranged to let Nanos and Billy Two know by moving the program to his right-hand pocket, a move that did not escape the contact's notice.

"You have backup, amigo?" the man asked.

"I have."

"I was told you are a careful man."

"You were told right."

"So I see," the man said. "Tell me, who do you like in this race?"

"The one dog," O'Toole said. For no particular reason other than the fact that the one dog always wore red, he had been playing the one all night. Of the first four races, he had won three. However, traditionally tourists played the one dog because they were informed that that box position won most of the time—and, in fact, it did. For that reason, O'Toole's payoffs had been small, and he was barely a hundred dollars ahead.

Still, he was winning, he thought with some satisfaction, when all he was doing was biding his time.

"Ah, I see," the Cuban said.

O'Toole knew what he was thinking. Another tourist—at least in his methods of playing the dogs. "I didn't come here to play the mutts, though," he said to the Cuban. "I came to do business."

"Ah, and that we shall do," the man said. "Come, my frien'. Let us talk…business. Come, I will buy you a hot dog."

O'Toole followed the Cuban to the snack bar, where they got hot dogs and plastic cups of ice-cold beer.

Gesturing with the hot dog, the Cuban said, "This is all you should eat in these places. The rest of the food is not fit for eating."

O'Toole saw his man look at the odds board. As the bell rang signifying that all betting windows were closed and the race was about to start, the Cuban said, "Now, tell me what you want."

"Is this the place—"

"Quickly, while the race is being run!"

"I'll need handguns, automatic weapons and probably some machine guns."

"None of those should be a problem. What about larger equipment?"

"I don't think so."

"Explosives?"

"No."

The Cuban looked at the monitor to see the dogs coming down the stretch toward the finish line. Quickly he told O'Toole what weapons he had available, and which of those weapons he would be able to supply more immediately than others.

"You will need time to make your choice," the man finished. "We will meet again."

"Where?"

"Here, Monday, for the matinee card."

O'Toole tried to arrange for an earlier get-together, but the Cuban wouldn't hear of it. He finished his hot dog, drained the beer cup and dumped it in the nearby trash barrel.

"Until then . . ."

"Yeah, but—"

"Please," the man said, cutting O'Toole off, "you and your friends will stay until the final race?"

"Of course."

"Until Monday, then," the man said and walked off into the crowd. Now that the race had finished, the people were back from their seats and the windows, and he quickly melted into the crowd.

O'Toole, Nanos and Billy Two stayed until the thirteenth race, as the Cuban had instructed them.

"How did you do?" Nanos asked Billy Two.

"I won a few hundred."

"And you?" he asked O'Toole.

"The same."

"Jesus," Nanos said, frowning. "I lost a hundred dollars."

"Could be worse," Billy Two said.

"How?"

"There could have been more losing Greek horses for you to bet on."

THE SOLDIERS OF BARRABAS were all gathered in Barrabas's hotel room. Nanos and Billy Two had taken a room at a motel. Claude Hayes was in the Hilton close by, while Lee Hatton had a room in the Sheraton, like Barrabas.

It was almost 1:00 a.m. Earlier Barrabas had ordered six bottles of beer, a bottle of wine and some ice.

Claude Hayes and Lee Hatton had been the last to arrive. Hayes was a big black ex-SEAL who was expert in underwater demolitions. Hatton was actually *Dr.* Hatton, and a very attractive dark-haired woman who had been forced on the SOBs initially and had since rightfully earned becoming a full-fledged member of the unit, many times over.

"All right, Liam," Barrabas asked, "what have we got?"

"Okay," O'Toole said, "aside from the shit he was trying to push me, he's got some AK-47s, AK-74s, M-16s and some Beretta AR-70s."

"What about machine guns?"

"M-60s, H&K 21s—"

"21s?" Barrabas asked, "or 21A1s?"

"21s," O'Toole replied, and Barrabas signaled for him to continue. "He's got some SIG 710s—"

Again Barrabas stopped him for some verification. He wanted to know if the SIGs were 710s or 710-3s.

"They're 710s, Colonel."

"Continue."

"With pistols we have more of a selection. Colts, Berettas, S&W's, Heckler & Koch, Rugers—"

"Suggestions, Liam," Barrabas said.

O'Toole thought for a moment, then reeled off the various considerations, which was why Barrabas liked to check things out with him. "I suggest we get M-16s for ourselves, Colonel, and outfit Berbick's men with either AK-47s, or AK-74s, whichever we can afford. Since we're not planning any direct contact with Trieste's army, I think a couple of M-60s would be sufficient. As for pistols, I think we should get them the Beretta 92s."

"What about the 92-Rs?" Nanos asked.

O'Toole looked at Nanos. The 92-R was designed to be fired as a normal automatic pistol, or in 3-round bursts. The problem with it was that when fired in 3-round bursts it required two hands to steady it. If Berbick's men were inexperienced, they'd have trouble controlling the 92-Rs. O'Toole explained all that, and Nanos nodded agreeably.

Barrabas liked the idea of the M-16s and M-60s. They were old friends from Nam. He had his own Beretta 93-R, so he'd let the others choose whatever handguns they wanted.

"All right, Liam," Barrabas said, "cut us a deal." He handed O'Toole the envelope with the money Jessup had given him.

The Irishman opened the envelope, counted the money and then stared at Barrabas. "Colonel—"

"Do the best you can," Barrabas said.

"Yeah," Alex the Greek said, "throw in some books of your poetry."

O'Toole gave Nanos a sour look and tucked the envelope into his pocket.

"When are you meeting again?" Barrabas asked.

"Monday, at the matinee card."

"Why Monday?"

"I couldn't get him any sooner," O'Toole said, shrugging.

"All right. What about a boat?"

"I'm meeting someone about that tomorrow."

"Where?"

O'Toole made a face and said, "In the Altamonte Mall, up at exit 48."

"Have you checked out the mall?"

"Yeah, it's huge."

"All right, and this time take Claude and Alex."

Barrabas was concerned about Billy Two's unpredictability among the crowds of people that would be at the mall. There wouldn't be the excitement of the dogs to occupy his mind.

"What about you?" O'Toole asked. "What's on your agenda?"

"I'm meeting Jessup again," Barrabas said. "We need landing coordinates."

"That's assuming we get a boat." O'Toole was still concerned about what little money they had to work with.

"You'll get a boat," Barrabas said. "I have every confidence in you."

"I appreciate that, Colonel."

"Get cleaned up, Liam, and then come back. I want you to go over the map with me. We've got to decide how and where we want to land."

"Yes, sir."

"Some of you already know that Nate Beck is not joining us, and that Bishop had a small job to do that had taken precedence over this mission." Barrabas inspected them with a cool look, and it was clear he wasn't offering any explanations. "All right, let's break this up," he added with finality. "We all have things to do tomorrow." He looked at Billy Two and said, "Billy, stick around your motel in case one of us has to call you. You can stay by the pool, but don't stray much farther than that."

The big Indian simply nodded.

"That's all," Barrabas finished, and as the SOBs filed out, Lee Hatton hung back, evidently wanting to talk to him.

"You didn't come up with anything for me to do, Colonel," she said after the others had left.

"Oh, sorry," he said. "You'll be coming with me, Lee. We have to look like a couple of tourists while we're meeting Jessup."

"Where are we going?"

"If I know Jessup," Barrabas said, "it'll be an alligator farm, or something. I'll call you in the morning."

"Yes, sir."

After Lee Hatton left, Barrabas opened one of the beers and nursed it. Again he went over the plan he and O'Toole had discussed. If what Walker Jessup had said about President Trieste's death squad was true, it seemed the only way to go. With what they had, there was no way they could launch a full offensive against Trieste's army. Their only chance was to penetrate Trieste's defenses, and that meant going up against his death squad, which could consist of how many men? Four? Five? Six? That was infinitely better than opposing his whole army with fifty men whose greatest asset was probably their loyalty.

He left the beer unfinished on the coffee table, spread out the maps he had brought and was still poring over them when O'Toole returned, and they jointly went over the maps and their strategy.

As Barrabas had told Jessup, it would have been easier to take a boat from Mexico to El Salvador than from Florida, but they'd just have to pick out a route and do the best they could.

They discussed going by plane, but of course the weapons they'd be carrying made commercial flights out of the question, and they certainly did not have the money to charter a plane privately. If they had they could even have taken the boat from Florida to Jamaica, and then flown into Honduras and walked into El Salvador. The current lack of funds also put a helicopter out of their reach.

Once they agreed that the approach would have to be by boat, they began discussing routes. O'Toole la-

mented the fact that they were buying their weapons in
Florida. As Barrabas had told Jessup, O'Toole mentioned how much easier it would have been to leave
from Mexico, taking the boat along the west coast of
Mexico and on to El Salvador.

They couldn't get near El Salvador from Florida,
unless they wanted to go through the Panama Canal,
and that wasn't feasible. The trip would be just too
long.

Finally, they decided that their best bet was to leave
from Key West like a bunch of fishermen. From there
they could go through the Yucatán Channel, land in
Honduras somewhere around Puerto Cortés or La
Ceiba, and then get a truck to the El Salvadoran border and walk in.

Barrabas would have to relay that information to
Jessup so that the fat man could find out if obtaining a
truck was possible, and enough men to carry the guns
and supplies in El Salvador.

Barrabas rolled up the maps and let O'Toole out,
wishing him luck in the morning at the mall.

"And be careful," he said as the Irishman stepped
into the hall, "don't get distracted by a sale."

O'Toole laughed and promised to be extra careful
about that.

Barrabas pulled out a pad and wrote a note to Jessup, then went down to the desk and asked the clerk to
put the envelope in the hotel safe for him.

If Barrabas knew the Fixer, he'd hear about the envelope within an hour.

THE ODDITY OF CENTRAL FLORIDA was that it was
made up of countless small cities. Nearly every exit a
motorist came to while driving along I-4 led off to an-

other small, self-contained city. They had their own police stations, their own fire departments, their own city halls—and some of them had their own shopping malls.

Exit 40 led off to the city of Altamonte Springs.

The Altamonte Mall had four major department stores and hundreds of smaller shops, restaurants and fast-food outlets. It also had two video arcades, one on the first level and one on the second. It was in the second-level arcade that O'Toole was to meet his contact about the boat.

O'Toole paused at the entrance to the arcade to change a couple of dollars into tokens for the machines. When he entered, he saw that the place was not crowded. It was very early, and the crowds had not yet filed into the mall in force. While he was trying to master a video baseball game called World Series according to the instructions, he felt someone come up beside him.

"Too bad they don't have any boat games," a voice said—a very familiar voice.

O'Toole straightened up and looked into the eyes of the same Cuban he had spoken to at the Sanford–Orlando Kennel Club the night before.

"You should have tol' me last night that you needed a boat, my friend," the man said.

"What is this, a game?"

"No game, amigo," the man said, spreading his hands. "*This* is a game. Do you like baseball?"

"As much as anyone."

"Ah, I love baseball. Here, I will show you. You bat and I will pitch, eh? I am very good at this game."

As it turned out, he was very good. O'Toole wasn't able to time the speed of the ball and was never able to hit it with the bat.

"I am very good, no?" the Cuban said. "A regular Mickey Mantle, eh?"

"More like Dwight Gooden," O'Toole said.

"Who?"

"Mickey Mantle was an outfielder," O'Toole said. "Dwight Gooden is a pitcher."

"I like the old ball players," the Cuban said. "I own many baseball cards."

"That's fine."

"Do you want to play again?"

"No," O'Toole said, "I'd rather talk about boats—that is, if you can talk about boats."

"I wear many hats, my frien'. Today, I am a dealer in boats. Tell me, what do you need?"

O'Toole told the Cuban what he needed. A boat large enough to carry the weapons he was buying, and six people.

"You will need a fishing boat of some kind," the man said. "One that can handle the deep water, but will not arouse any undue attention. Do you want to buy or rent?"

"Rent."

"Ah," he said, "that means you need someone to drive the boat so they can bring it back."

"That's right."

"That will be expensive."

O'Toole took a deep breath and said, "Money is not a problem."

"*Bueno,*" the man answered. "I will see what I can do for you."

As the man started to turn away O'Toole asked, "Whoa, whoa, what about the weapons?"

"As I say before," the Cuban said, "I am a man of many hats. Today I am a dealer in boats. Monday afternoon I will be a dealer in arms."

"But we could—"

"Tsk, tsk." The Cuban clucked his tongue. "There are procedures we must follow. We are very organized, you see. Surely a man such as yourself understands procedure."

"Oh, sure," O'Toole said, "I understand procedure."

"Until Monday, then," the man said, and left the arcade.

O'Toole walked out right behind him and waited until the Cuban had gone into the mall proper from the wing where the arcade was. O'Toole found Alex Nanos standing in front of a B. Dalton bookstore. Claude Hayes was across the way in front of a record outlet, his head bopping to the music.

O'Toole approached Nanos, and when Hayes saw them together he crossed over.

O'Toole could still see the Cuban and pointed him out to Nanos.

"Isn't that the same guy—" Nanos started to say.

"Yes, he's the same as last night. Follow him and see where he goes."

"Why?"

"I don't like the feel of things, Alex—now go! Follow him!"

"I'm gone," Nanos said. He had the keys to the rental car in his pocket. O'Toole and Hayes would make their own way back to their hotels.

"What's going on, Liam?" Hayes asked.

"I don't like the idea that I got the same contact for arms and a boat. Somewhere along the way I think we're being set up."

"I thought your contacts—"

"My contacts put me on to other contacts," O'Toole said. "As of now, we're dealing with people we don't know. There's always the danger of a rip-off when you do that. Come on, let's get back and talk to the colonel."

"He and the doc are probably off meeting Jessup."

"We'll wait in his room," O'Toole said. "I've got a bad feeling, and I want him to know about it."

AT THAT MOMENT Barrabas and Lee Hatton were at a place called Fun 'n' Wheels, a small theme park with water slides, car rides, skeet ball and arcade games.

That morning Barrabas had presented himself at the front desk and asked for the envelope he had left in the safe. Without batting an eyelash the young clerk—a woman but not the same woman he had talked to yesterday—handed him an envelope. When he opened it, it simply said, Fun 'n' Wheels.

The park was located on International Drive, tucked in behind a fast-food outlet and a hotel. When they arrived, they walked around, bought some tokens and played skeet ball until they had a handful of prize tickets. Hatton turned out to be fairly good at the game, and the higher she scored the more prize tickets came out of the machine. When she combined hers with Barrabas's, they had quite a handful.

"What would you like?" Barrabas asked her, with his arm around her waist. To anyone looking on they appeared to be a husband and wife on vacation. Barrabas had even purchased a loud shirt from the hotel gift shop and was wearing it hanging loosely outside his pants. It also served very well to cover his Beretta 93-R.

"I want the orange toucan," she said, then turned to the attendant. "Do I have enough tickets?"

The young man counted them up and said, "Yes, ma'am, and you'll still have some left over." He smiled at her and handed over the colorful toucan.

She accepted it happily, and then turned and handed her remaining tickets to a little girl who was standing nearby with her mother.

"Oh, how nice," the girl's mother said. "What do you say?" she reminded the child with a fond look.

The little girl, who was about eight years old, looked up at Hatton with glowing eyes. "Thank you very much." Then she turned to her mother and said excitedly, "Mommy, now I can get the monkey."

"Yes you can, dear," the woman said, smiling her thanks to Hatton and Barrabas.

"That was nice of you," Barrabas said to Hatton as they walked away.

"Why not?" she asked. "I've got what I wanted." She held up her toucan as if it were an Olympic medal.

"Yes, you did."

He still had his arm around her, his hand on her slender waist. To match his appearance as much as she could, she had purchased a tank top that was purple and had darker purple splotches on it. It did not quite come down to the belt of her shorts, and her navel was showing. Barrabas was more aware that she was a beautiful woman than he had been for some time.

"Let's go over by the water slides," he said.

"I didn't think that would interest you," Hatton said playfully.

"It's near the snack bar," he explained. "That's probably where we'll find Jessup."

His words brought back to her the real reason they were there. They walked over to the snack bar together, and found that Jessup was not hard to spot. The fat man was seated at a table by himself, eating a hot dog that was dripping with onions and ketchup, while he himself dripped with perspiration. Like Barrabas, he had affected a gaudy-looking shirt, this one a floral pattern in painful reds, yellows and oranges. A wide-brimmed straw hat was perched atop his head.

"Sit right here, dear," Barrabas said to Lee as they reached Jessup's table. "I'll get you something cold to drink."

"I could use a hot dog," she said.

"All right."

Hatton sat opposite Jessup while Barrabas went off. She cast a careful look around, and then eyed Jessup curiously until Barrabas came back with one hot dog and two cups of Coke.

"I see you're enjoying yourself," Jessup remarked with a look at the toucan on the table next to Hatton.

"She has good hand-to-eye coordination," Barrabas said. "What do you have for me?"

"Coordinates," Jessup said, pushing some napkins over to Barrabas. Barrabas picked up the top one, saw the numbers written on it and made a show of wiping his mouth. He crumpled it then and put it in his shirt pocket.

"Also, I don't see any problems with any of your other requests."

"Good."

"Have you got a boat yet?" Jessup asked.

"We're working on it. Any further word on the strength of Trieste's army?"

"Uh, no, not yet."

Whatever the problem was, Barrabas had given up on getting accurate information about Trieste's army. It didn't much matter, since they didn't intend to try to take them on in any kind of force.

"Any chance of coming up with more money?"

"Not a prayer," Jessup said.

At that point a particularly large young woman came shooting down the water slide on a plastic sled and landed with a great splash, which sent a spray of water raining down on Jessup, Hatton and Barrabas.

"Now I know why no one else was sitting here," Jessup said glumly. Then he brightened and said, "Actually, that was pretty refreshing."

Barrabas looked at Hatton, who was popping a last bite into her mouth.

"I think we've had enough fun for one day," Barrabas said.

"When you're ready to move," Jessup said, "leave me a message at the drop. If I get anything for you, I'll do the same."

"All right," Barrabas said, already standing. Hatton picked up her toucan and joined him.

"Nice bird," Jessup said to her.

"Thanks."

As Barrabas and Hatton walked away, Jessup reached over and picked up Barrabas's untouched soft drink.

Barrabas and Hatton walked to the parking lot, where they'd left their rental car parked right next to the miniature golf course. When they got in, Barrabas took the napkin from his pocket and handed it to her.

"Write that down legibly somewhere."

She took a pad out of her purse and copied the numbers down, then tore the napkin into tiny little pieces. As they pulled onto the highway she opened her window and allowed the pieces to flutter out.

Hatton found the ensuing minutes awkward. She was not often paired with Barrabas, and didn't quite know what she was supposed to say or do. Finally she figured that Barrabas was probably thinking, and since she didn't want to interrupt his train of thought she just sat back, hugging her prize as they rode to the hotel in silence.

When they got back to Barrabas's room, they found O'Toole and Hayes waiting for them with Billy Two. Barrabas removed his Beretta 93-R from his belt and set it down on the writing desk, then turned to O'Toole, who was staring at Hatton's stuffed toucan.

"Where's Alex?" Barrabas asked, casting alternating glances at both Hayes and O'Toole.

Hayes looked at O'Toole.

"I had him follow the Cuban from the mall, Colonel."

"Another Cuban?" Barrabas said. "Well, I guess that's not surprising."

"No, sir," O'Toole replied, "the same Cuban. The same man I talked to last night about the guns."

"We're dealing with the same guy on the boat?" Barrabas asked.

O'Toole nodded.

"Why did you have Alex follow him?"

"Something doesn't feel right to me, Colonel," O'Toole said. "I had Alex tail him, and called Billy to pick Claude and me up."

"What do you expect him to find?"

"I don't know."

"What do you think?"

"I smell a rip-off."

"Why?"

O'Toole frowned. "I did mention that money was not a problem for us."

"But it is," Hatton said.

O'Toole looked at her. "He didn't have to know that."

"Who's ripping who off?" she asked.

"Never mind, Lee," Barrabas said to her. "I think it's a good call." He looked at O'Toole and asked, "How long ago was this, Liam?"

"About an hour, Colonel," O'Toole said. "Alex should be back any time now."

They all hoped so.

3

It was difficult to tail someone when they knew the city and you didn't. For that reason Alex Nanos found that he had to stay closer to the Cuban than he would normally have.

He almost lost him right in the parking lot, not sure which way the man was exiting. He finally spotted the man's beat-up Pontiac Grand Prix leaving the parking lot on the Palm Springs Road side, and hurried to fall in behind him.

Palm Springs Road was not a major road, but it was apparently well enough travelled that Nanos was able to keep another car between him and the Cuban at all times.

When they reached State Road 426, the Cuban made a right turn and continued on until he reached the junction of 17 and 92. There he made a left and Nanos stayed with him. Both roads—426 and 17–92—were major thoroughfares, and again, although he had to stay closer than he would have liked, there were enough vehicles on the roads so he wouldn't become conspicuous.

Signs along the way indicated to Nanos that they were heading toward Lake Mary and Sanford. As it turned out, their destination was actually right between the two.

Nanos saw the Grand Prix turn right and enter the parking lot of a huge flea market complex. He tramped down on his gas pedal and hurried into the parking lot before he lost sight of his quarry.

He needn't have bothered.

There were so many cars in the lot that it was almost impossible to see where the Cuban had parked his Grand Prix.

Remaining calm, Nanos began to drive around the parking lot, looking for the green Grand Prix. When he finally found it, there wasn't another parking spot next to it. He found one about seven rows away, where the surface was dirt instead of blacktop, and then walked back. Playing a hunch, he simply headed for the nearest entrance, figuring that maybe the Cuban was connected enough to rate his own parking spot.

The inside of the flea market was even worse than the outside. It was divided by aisles, and each aisle was marked with a letter. The letters ran from A to S. That left nineteen aisles for him to look through, as well as some smaller rows that weren't large enough to earn letters of their own. In addition to that, there was an enclosed smaller market of three rows in the center of the complex, where the rents were presumably higher.

Junk, Nanos thought as he wandered through the market. The booths sold antiques, jewelry, books, baseball cards, lamps, furniture. There was even one that sold knives, throwing stars—called *shuriken*—and bows and arrows. As he continued on, he couldn't understand why so many booths sold the same things. How many of these people could make a living selling the same merchandise?

When Nanos came to one of the snack bars, he ordered a hamburger, a big cup of string fries and a beer.

He sat down at a booth somebody must have stolen from a diner and wondered if he'd get lucky and have the Cuban wander by.

After he finished eating, he found a pay phone and called Barrabas's hotel.

"IT'S ALEX," Nanos said when Barrabas picked up the phone.

"Where are you?' Barrabas asked.

"At a flea market near a place called Sanford. Do you know where that is?"

"Sanford, yes, I think so." Barrabas looked over to where O'Toole was sitting. The others had left. "Exactly where is this flea market located?"

"On something called 17–92. It's north of Lake Mary and south of Sanford."

"Where's the Cuban?"

"He's in here somewhere."

"You lost him?"

"Nah, he's in here somewhere," Nanos said. "I can see his car from here. I could sit on it, but that won't accomplish what Liam wants."

"No, it won't," Barrabas said. "Hold on, Alex." He looked at O'Toole and said, "Liam, Nanos lost the Cuban in a flea market."

Barrabas heard Nanos's voice come over the phone complaining, "I didn't lose him!"

"A flea market?" O'Toole said. "What do they sell there besides fleas?"

"What do they sell there?" Barrabas asked Nanos.

"Stuff, they sell stuff!" Nanos said. "Hell, pots and pans, jewelry, comic books, paperback books, furniture, baseball cards..."

As the Greek reeled off the items, Barrabas relayed them to O'Toole. Barrabas was hoping the Cuban might have said something that would give O'Toole some idea of why he'd be at a flea market.

"Wait, stop," O'Toole said. "Colonel, did he say baseball cards?"

"He did," Barrabas confirmed.

"That's it," O'Toole said. "The Cuban's a baseball fanatic—an *old* baseball fanatic. He collects old baseball cards!"

"Alex, Liam says the Cuban collects baseball cards. Look at all the baseball card tables."

"Okay."

"Get back to me."

"Okay," Nanos said ponderingly. "Hot damn, baseball cards..."

Nanos hung up and shook his head. A grown man collecting baseball cards. What next?

He started walking around, stopping at the baseball card booths. He didn't know how many there were and was just about to ask someone when he spotted the Cuban.

The man was at a baseball card booth, only he wasn't there looking at cards—he was behind the table, selling them!

"WHAT ABOUT ANOTHER contact?" O'Toole asked Barrabas.

"Do they grow on trees?" Barrabas asked him. "Look how long it took you to come up with this one—and that's not to criticize you. I'm just saying it won't be so easy to go elsewhere."

"So what do we do?"

"We find out if the Cuban is in fact planning to rip us off."

"And if he is?"

"We rip him off first."

"You mean take the guns and the boat?"

"That's one way to beat the money shortage, isn't it?"

"Yeah," the Irishman said with a grin, "it sure is."

The phone rang at that point and Barrabas picked it up. It was Nanos, with the news that he had found the Cuban.

"He's what?" Barrabas said. He wasn't sure he had heard the Greek correctly.

"He's selling baseball cards, Colonel," Nanos said. "He's got his own booth."

"All right," Barrabas said. "Hang around, Alex, and keep your ears open. Find out what you can. Uh, do you know anything about baseball cards?"

"Colonel, I grew up in a small fishing village in Greece," Nanos reminded him. "Sponge divers don't get their faces on sports cards—at least, not yet."

"Yeah, right," Barrabas said. "Okay, then just watch and listen and see what you come up with."

"How long do you want me to stay?"

"I don't know," Barrabas said. "What time does that place close?"

"I get the picture," Nanos said. "I'll have some more string fries."

"You do that. Talk to you later."

Barrabas hung up and looked at O'Toole.

"So?"

"The Cuban is selling baseball cards."

"*Selling* baseball cards?" O'Toole said, smiling. "Well, the son of a bitch did say that he wore a lot of hats. I guess he wasn't kidding, was he?"

"I've got a map of the Central American coast here," Barrabas said. "Let's check those coordinates the fat man gave me."

NANOS WANDERED around, eating another cupful of string fries, trying to think of an approach. Finally he just walked right up to the table and started leafing through some baseball card books. He saw some names he recognized—Hank Aaron, Mickey Mantle—and some that he didn't—Kirk Gibson, Jack Clark, Roger Clemens.

"You in'erested in cards?" the Cuban asked.

"I used to collect when I was a kid," Nanos said.

"If you have any of the old cards left, I buy them from you."

"Ah, I think my mother got rid of them when I moved out."

"Ah, too bad."

While Nanos was leafing through the books, a man came along and joined the Cuban behind the table. The two greeted each other as though they were more than just partners in a baseball card booth.

Nanos noticed that behind the Cuban the tent flaps gaped a bit, and beyond he could see the parking lot. A man could hear a lot from there.

"Not buying?" the Cuban said to him as he turned away.

"I'm going to check with my mother first," Nanos said.

He dumped the remains of his string fries into a trash barrel and found the nearest exit.

BARRABAS ANSWERED the knock on his door and found Nanos standing outside.

"I'm home."

"Come on in."

Nanos entered and winked at O'Toole. "Good tip about the baseball cards," Nanos said.

"What'd you find out?"

Nanos didn't bother telling Barrabas and O'Toole how long he had to crouch behind that baseball card booth between two trash dumpsters that conveniently hid him from sight. He'd had to listen to a lot of mindless bullshit that ranged from the size of some tourist girl's tits—although he did peek when he heard that—to the price of an Eddie Davis rookie card, whoever that was, before something of real interest was finally said.

"It's a rip-off, all right," he said.

"When?" Barrabas asked.

"When they deliver."

Barrabas looked at O'Toole. "That means they *will* deliver."

"And then try to kill us."

"That's the key word," Barrabas said. " 'Try.' "

"It sure would help if we knew where to put our hands on this guy."

"There's something else that might help," Nanos said.

"Oh yeah? What's that?" Barrabas asked.

"I found out the Cuban's name."

"What is it?"

"Miguel Rivera."

"How does that help us?" O'Toole asked. "He sure won't be listed in the phone book."

"We don't need a listing," Nanos said. "I followed the silly bastard home."

"Wha—" O'Toole said.

Nanos grinned and said, "I know exactly where he lives."

WHEN O'TOOLE MET the Cuban at the dog track on Monday afternoon, his backup was Hayes and Billy Two. Nanos couldn't go because the Cuban had seen him at the flea market.

"Well, my frien'," Miguel Rivera said as he approached O'Toole. "How are you doing today?"

The prices for the fifth race had just gone up on the odds board.

"Not too good."

"Ah, the one dogs are not treating you well, eh?"

"I guess not."

"So, have you decided what you want?"

"Yes." O'Toole handed Rivera his program and said, "Look at the eighth race."

Rivera turned to the eighth race in the program and saw what O'Toole had written there. He nodded, put the program in his left-hand pocket and took out his own. He turned to the fifth race and wrote something down, then handed the program to O'Toole.

"The fifth race, my frien'."

O'Toole turned to that race and looked at the price the Cuban had written down.

"That's way out of line," he said, and they proceeded to dicker, even though neither one of them intended to keep any kind of cash deal they made.

Finally they agreed on a price, and O'Toole asked, "What about the boat? Can we talk about that now?"

"Sure, my frien', sure," the Cuban said. "We can talk about the boat."

Sure, you lying thief, O'Toole thought, but kept a straight if somewhat peeved face.

They bartered about the boat for a while, and then agreed on a price. If everything had been on the up-and-up the SOBs wouldn't have had nearly enough money.

After they had finished their phony bickering, the Cuban asked where O'Toole was staying. O'Toole told him, because there was no harm in that. Rivera and his people wouldn't try anything until they had the money, and he was the only one of the SOBs who was staying there.

"I will be in touch," Rivera said. "Of course, you and your people will stay until the last race?"

"Of course," O'Toole agreed.

"Play the five horse in that race, then," the Cuban advised. "He cannot lose."

"I'll remember."

As Rivera left, Hayes and Billy Two came over to O'Toole.

"Is it all over?" Hayes asked.

"Yes," O'Toole said, "it's all settled. We're asshole buddies, now."

Hayes made a face. "I've always hated that phrase."

"He want us to stay until the last race?" Billy Two asked.

"Yep."

"Are we?"

"What do you think?"

"Good," Billy Two said, throwing his program into a nearby trash receptacle. "The gods aren't with me today, anyway."

THAT EVENING they met in Hatton's room.

"All right," Barrabas said. "The guns are coming. Lee, I want you to go to Key West and rent a boat."

"Key West?" she asked.

He nodded. "That's where we'll leave from."

"What do I use for money?"

Barrabas looked at O'Toole, who took out the envelope of money.

"Keep some for handguns," Barrabas said to him. "We'll need them for the delivery night. Give her the rest."

O'Toole took some of the money out and passed Hatton the rest.

"What kind of boat?" she asked.

"Something that would be used for deep-sea fishing."

"Wouldn't Alex or Claude be better suited for this?"

"Yes, they would, but I need them here. Alex is the contact and Claude . . . well, he's scary looking as hell and you, my dear doctor, are not."

"Colonel," she said, "I do believe that's the nicest thing you've ever said to me."

Barrabas wasn't sure, but suspected that she was right.

THREE DAYS LATER O'Toole found a message waiting for him at the front desk. He took it to his room, read it and immediately called Barrabas.

"I've got a meeting."

"Come on over."

When O'Toole arrived at the colonel's room, the other SOBs were also there.

"Does he have the guns?" Barrabas asked.

"Near as I can figure."

"And a boat?"

"Probably," O'Toole said. "He'll probably claim that he wants me to examine the guns first before we agree on a delivery site."

"When does he want to meet?"

"Wednesday night. Midnight." O'Toole gave the word all the drama it deserved.

"Where?"

"In the parking lot of the flea market."

"All right," Barrabas said. "Claude, we'll need a van. How about renting one?"

"Yes, sir."

"Lee's rented us a boat."

"What kind?" Nanos asked. He was from a poor Greek fishing family and could sail anything. Of course, the boat Hatton had rented would be no sailboat, but then Nanos was a coast guard vet, as well.

"I don't know, Alex," Barrabas said. "Why don't you call her and find out?"

Nanos could just imagine Hatton trying to describe the boat over the phone.

"I'll wait until we see it."

"Right. Once Claude has rented the van, we'll go and pay a visit on Mr. Rivera."

"When?" O'Toole asked.

"Tomorrow is only Tuesday," Barrabas said. "So we'll be a little early for our appointment."

FROM THE FLEA MARKET Nanos had followed Miguel Rivera to a house in Longwood. On Tuesday night he drove the rented van with Barrabas sitting next to him and the other SOBs in the back. They all had .45s that Barrabas had had O'Toole purchase for them locally.

Nanos stopped the van half a block from Rivera's house. They would continue on foot from there. The neighborhood was middle class; the homes were comfortable, well kept and about twenty years old.

"All right," Barrabas said, "Alex and Billy Two will come with me. Liam, Claude, keep a sharp eye out."

Both men nodded.

As Barrabas, Nanos and Billy Two left the van, they heard O'Toole say to Hayes, "Would you like to hear some poetry?"

They were approaching the house when Nanos whispered, "The back door, Colonel. It's darker in the back."

They moved around to the back where they found a sliding glass door, and a pool door to a bathroom.

"The pool door," Barrabas said. "Billy?"

Billy Two took out a big bowie knife and used it to slip the lock on the pool door.

"Who else is inside?" Barrabas asked Nanos.

"No one," Nanos said. "He lives alone."

"In a house like this?"

"Maybe his wife left him."

"Smart lady."

Barrabas went in first, followed by Nanos and then the big Indian. They found the bedroom, where Miguel Rivera was snoring healthily.

"All right," Barrabas said to Nanos, "wake him up."

Nanos went to the bed and turned on one of the end table lamps.

"Let's go, sleeping beauty," he called out, "rise and shine."

Rivera opened his eyes, squinting against the light, and said, "What the hell—"

"Hello, Miguel," Nanos said, sitting on the bed in front of him. "Remember me?"

"Yes?" the Cuban said, then his eyes focused and he said "You!" in a totally different tone of voice.

"I thought you might remember me," Nanos said.

"What are you doin' here?"

"We came for our guns," Barrabas said.

"Your guns?" Rivera said. "I don't know—"

"You made a deal with a friend of ours," Barrabas explained.

"But—but we agreed to meet tomorrow night."

"You agreed to meet tomorrow night," Nanos told him. "But we prefer to do business tonight."

"But—but I—we're not ready."

"That's okay," Nanos said. "We are."

"I can't—"

"Tell us where the guns are," Nanos demanded.

"I can't tell you that!" Rivera said, looking shocked at the prospect.

"That's okay," Nanos said. "We're reasonable. You don't have to tell me—tell him!"

At that moment Billy Two stepped through the doorway and into the light. On his face he wore his war paint, red streaks down each cheek.

"Full-blooded Osage," Nanos said, "and he's on the warpath, as you can see." Nanos looked at Rivera again and said with emphasis, "Now, where are the guns?"

"I—I can't—"

"Billy!" Barrabas said.

Billy Two stepped forward and towered over the bed. He took out his bowie knife, and let the Cuban have a good look at it.

"Hey, get him away from me," Rivera shouted.

Billy grinned and leaned over the man.

"Get him away!" Rivera shrieked.

Billy used the knife to slice off the man's pajama top.

"Hey," Rivera shouted at Nanos, "this Indian's crazy!"

"I know," Nanos said, smiling, "and that's the only thing we like about him."

From that point on, it didn't take long to find out what they wanted, and when Barrabas, Nanos and Billy Two returned to the van they brought company with them.

They pushed Rivera into the back with Hayes, and O'Toole and Billy Two climbed in after him.

"Did you hurt him?" O'Toole asked.

"Didn't have to," Nanos said. "Billy Two scared it out of him." He shut the car door.

O'Toole looked at Rivera. "I don't blame you, Miguel," he said, switching his gaze to Billy Two. "He scares me, too, when he looks like that."

Nanos got behind the wheel of the van and started the engine.

Barrabas nodded and said, "Let's go and get our guns."

They followed Rivera's directions to a warehouse not far from Orlando Airport. Once it had been part of an old airport, and now it was empty. According to Rivera, it was used for storing guns, cars, drugs or whatever his associates happened to be running.

Nanos pulled the van off the road, stopped a hundred yards from the warehouse and leaned on the steering wheel.

"Do you think he's telling the truth, Colonel?"

"I think he's too scared not to." Barrabas turned and asked, "What do you think, Liam?"

Liam O'Toole looked down at Miguel Rivera, who was lying on the floor of the van with Claude Hayes's and Billy Two's feet resting on him.

"From the look on his face, Colonel," O'Toole said, "I'd say he was telling the truth."

"All right, Billy," Barrabas said. "Time to go and take a look."

Billy Two, aside from the natural abilities inherited from his ancestors, was an expert in guerrilla warfare. As such, when it was time to scout out a location, he was the man who went in first.

"Yes sir," Billy Two said. He was out the back door and on his way in seconds.

Rivera started to get up, but Claude Hayes slapped him back down to the floor with both feet.

"Not yet, friend," Hayes said. "If my Indian buddy comes back with bad news, there won't be any reason for you to get up—ever again."

BILLY TWO MOVED across the field like a cat, his swiftness and grace in direct contradiction to his bulk. When he reached the building, he flattened himself against the side and listened. From inside he heard the sound of voices. With the extra awareness given him by Hawk Spirit, he was also able to detect a faint smell of cigarette smoke in the air.

He crept along the wall until he came to a bank of windows that had all been blacked out. He passed them, then he reached another set of blackened windows. Again he moved on and continued in that fashion until he had gone around three quarters of the building. Finally, he found a window that had a small piece missing from its pane. It was barely large enough for his eye, but he bent to put his eye right next to it. There was light inside, and he could see crates. Of course, he had had no way of knowing what was in the crates, but they served to indicate that something was inside—something and someone.

He stood with his back to the window, listening intently. He could not see how many men were inside, and so he would have to depend on the senses given him by Hawk Spirit for an accurate count.

Next he checked the front doors. They were corrugated metal, old and weathered.

Satisfied, he moved away from the building and made his way across the field back to the van. He entered the van from the back and sat down. Absently he placed one foot on Miguel Rivera's stomach.

"How does it look, Billy?" Barrabas asked, turning in his seat.

"There are crates inside," Billy Two said, "and at least four men."

"Did you see them?" Alex Nanos asked.

Billy Two looked at Nanos. "There are four of them."

Nanos looked at Barrabas, and the mercenary leader knew what the Greek was thinking.

"Hawk Spirit."

Well, Barrabas thought, the big Osage's record was certainly excellent—not perfect, but then who was?

"All right," Barrabas said, "we'll go in. Billy, what about entry?"

"Front door only, sir. We could go in through a window, but it'd have to be shattered."

"Too noisy. It would alert them too quickly."

"Suggestion?"

"Right through the front doors," Billy said. "They're corrugated metal, but old. They won't hold."

"Oh, Jesus," Nanos groaned. "Are we going to get another car rental agency mad at us?"

Barrabas gave him a blank look and Nanos said, "Oh yes, we are."

FOUR MEN SAT playing poker inside the warehouse. Three of them were smoking. In one corner there were four cots all made up for sleeping, but the men didn't appear to be prepared for sleeping. They were wearing guns.

"Call," one man said, throwing a dollar into the pot. "What have you got?"

The man across from him said, "Three lovely kings."

"Shit," the man said who had called. "I finally made three of a kind and they got to be deuces."

"Better than what I had," one of the other men remarked, dropping his cards on the table.

"Who deals?" the fourth man asked.

"Christ," the man with the deuces said, "can't you ever remember? You deal!"

"All right, all right, take it easy," the dealer said, gathering up the cards.

"Hey, how big a score did Rivera say this was gonna be?" the winner of that pot asked.

"He said they claimed money was no problem," the second man said. "There should be plenty in it for us."

"Hey, you hear something?" the dealer asked. He'd only dealt out four cards, and he paused, his head cocked in a listening attitude.

"No," the second man said. He'd already picked up his cards and saw that they were all the same, three aces. "Hurry up and deal, will ya?" he said.

"I hear something, I tell ya!"

"I don't—" the second man said, but then he did. It sounded like a motor, and it was getting closer—

At that moment the corrugated front doors squealed and crashed open, and a van came hurtling into the warehouse.

The poker table had been set up in a direct line with the front door, so that all four men had to scramble to get out of the way of the van. The front of the vehicle slammed into the table, sending it and its contents flying about the room.

The back doors of the van opened before it had even come to a stop. Billy Two, Claude Hayes and Liam O'Toole emerged, holding their .45s in front of them.

Alex Nanos opened his door and jumped out, while Barrabas did the same on his side.

"Don't!" Liam O'Toole shouted as one of the four poker players grabbed for a gun he was wearing under his arm, but the man didn't listen. O'Toole fired, and the man staggered back, his arms flailing about. He was dead before he hit the ground.

"Nobody move!" Barrabas shouted.

A second man made the same mistake as the first. He tried to pull his gun and Barrabas fired his Beretta 93-R. His shot struck the man in the chest, puncturing his heart.

The other two quickly put their hands over their heads with a chorus of "Hey, hey, don't shoot, don't shoot!"

O'Toole and Nanos rushed them and divested them of their guns.

"Look around!" Barrabas ordered.

Billy Two and Claude Hayes began moving toward the crates that sat along the walls, each picking up a crowbar along the way. They started to pry the crates open, looking for the guns.

"They've got everything here," Hayes said. "I got cigarettes."

"I've got what looks like antiques."

"All this stuff must be hot, and they sell it at flea markets," Barrabas said.

"Does that mean there are some hot baseball cards in here somewhere?" Alex Nanos asked.

"I don't know about baseball cards," Barrabas said, "but there had better be some guns."

Barrabas looked over at the van then and saw Miguel Rivera half fall out of the back. "Miguel!" he called.

Rivera staggered to his feet and looked at Barrabas.

"Come and join the party."

Rivera looked at the ruined door, and then at Barrabas again.

"Don't even think about it, Rivera," Barrabas said. "Come on over here."

Slowly Rivera began walking toward Barrabas.

"Portable television sets!" Claude Hayes shouted.

"Stereo cassette players!" Billy Two sang out.

Liam O'Toole had joined the search, leaving the two men under Nanos's gun, and now he opened a crate and stared inside incredulously.

"Hell," he called out, "you won't believe this. Stuffed animals."

"Come here," Barrabas said to Rivera, putting one arm around him and prodding him in the belly with the Beretta 93-R. "Where are the guns?"

Rivera stared at Barrabas with fear in his eyes. "You—you're gonna kill me anyway," he stammered.

"Even if that were true," Barrabas said, "there are all kinds of different ways to die. I could shoot you in the head and do it quick, or in the belly and let you bleed to death. Or, I could give you to Billy over there and let him cut your heart out.''

Rivera's eyes popped and he said, "All right, all right, I'll show you.''

"Aw," Claude Hayes said, "I was just starting to enjoy this. It's almost like Christmas morning.''

Barrabas prodded Rivera in the back with his gun and followed the Cuban to a stack of crates.

"Is this them?" Barrabas asked.

Rivera nodded jerkily.

"Claude!"

Hayes and Billy Two came over, lifted a crate off the top and pried it open.

"Bingo," Hayes said. "We got guns, Colonel.''

"Load them up.''

Barrabas covered Rivera and the other two men while the SOBs loaded the guns onto the van, checking each crate first. In all, they had four crates.

"There's more, Colonel," O'Toole said.

"Just take what we need, Liam.''

"Yes, sir.''

When the crates were loaded Hayes, Billy Two and O'Toole climbed into the back with them.

"Colonel," Nanos said, "what's going to keep these fellas from coming after us?''

"They're going to be busy moving all this stuff before the police get here.''

"Aw," one of the men said, "you wouldn't.''

"Yes," Nanos said, "he would.''

"Adios," Barrabas said. "Nice doing business with you.''

4

By taking turns behind the wheel of the van the Soldiers of Barrabas covered the more than four hundred miles between Orlando and Key West in less than six hours. Alex Nanos was amazed by how much a driver could exceed the speed limit in Florida and not be stopped.

At the Key West Hilton, Lee Hatton had already reserved three rooms for them. She had hoped to get them on the same floor, but did not make an issue of it. Barrabas was on her floor, the third, while the others were on the eleventh.

On the way to Key West they had stopped and bought fishing gear with what was left of the money Walker Jessup had given them, so at least they'd look like fisherman. Nanos, having grown up in a fishing village, was the expert and did the purchasing.

"It's got to look like we're going to do deep-water fishing, Alex," Barrabas told him.

"Hell, Colonel," Nanos had said, "maybe we can, just to while away the time."

Also, before leaving, Barrabas had had one more sit-down with Jessup. This time they had met at a place called Gatorland Farm.

Jessup had gotten there first, and when Barrabas arrived, the fat man was sampling some of the alligator meat for sale in the snack shop.

"You know," he said to Barrabas, "they say it tastes like fried chicken, and it really does. Have some?"

"No, thanks." Barrabas had eaten things to survive that would have turned Walker Jessup's stomach—no small feat—but he didn't see any reason to add alligator to the list if he did not have to.

"Let's walk," he said to Jessup, who took his little cardboard dish of alligator meat with him as they started out.

"Are we all set at the other end?" he asked Jessup.

"There'll be a man waiting for you at those landing coordinates I gave you," Jessup assured him. "He'll have some Miskitos to help carry the stuff when you reach the border between Honduras and El Salvador."

"The Miskito Indians are Contras," Barrabas said. "I thought they weren't going to be involved."

"These Indians won't be involved. They'll just be there as beasts of burden. Did you get all the weapons you needed?" Jessup asked.

"Everything."

"With the money I gave you?" Jessup looked surprised.

Barrabas did not give the fat man the benefit of any expression when he said, "We economized."

"What about a boat?"

"Don't worry."

"Where are you leaving from?"

"You don't have to know that," Barrabas said. "We'll be leaving here tomorrow morning. We should be at the rendezvous point within a week to ten days."

They had four hundred miles to travel from Orlando to Key West, almost nine hundred from Key West to the Gulf of Honduras. After they met their contact, they'd have a hundred miles to do by truck to El Salvador, and then who knew how far to walk before they finally reached Berbick.

"Just have your man standing by—and tell him not to leave even if he thinks we're late!"

"He'll be there," Jessup said, popping a piece of meat into his mouth.

"He'd better be. I'm not looking forward to all this traveling, Jessup. I'll frown on it even more if it's all for nothing."

"Don't worry," Jessup told him, "it won't be."

"Let me ask you a question."

"What?"

"If you had so little money to give us for supplies, how do you expect to pay us when we're finished?"

"Oh, yes, well…" Jessup paused to lick some grease from his fingers.

"Don't stall me, fat man!" Barrabas said.

"I'm not stalling, no, no," said Jessup. "It's just that your, ah, fee will depend a lot on the, uh, success of this mission. And of course, you needn't worry on that count because you've always been successful, haven't you?"

"You'd better hope our record stays intact, fat man," Barrabas had said as he'd poked Walker Jessup in the chest with a forefinger that was like an iron spike.

Remembering that occasion as they drove up to the Key West hotel still had Barrabas shaking his head. He wondered about Jessup's motivation in life and could only come up with a shrug for an answer.

The hotel had a parking garage, and after Barrabas had checked them all in they pulled into the garage with the van.

"Okay," Barrabas told them, turning in his seat, "I don't expect us to be here that long, but with the stuff we've got in this van, one of us is going to have to be out here at all times."

"You mean one of *us*, don't you, Colonel?" Alex Nanos said with a smile.

"That's right," Barrabas agreed, "one of you—and Hatton will take a turn."

None of them said anything in response to that. It had been decided long ago by them and by Lee Hatton that she was one of them, and shared in all the scut work. If there was any glory, she'd share in that, as well.

"Divvy it up among you," Barrabas suggested, "starting now," and he got out of the van. "Meet me in my room in an hour," he added, before walking away.

He went up to his room with his bag and then phoned Lee Hatton. "The boys are in the garage dividing up the watch time. You'll get what's left over." If one of them was absent when watches were being set, it was understood—and accepted by all—that that person would get what was left over.

"No problem," she said.

"Be in my room in an hour."

"Yes, sir."

He hung up and went to shower.

AN HOUR LATER they were all in Barrabas's room except Claude Hayes, who had drawn the first watch on the van.

"Lee, you take Alex to have a look at the boat and then get back here. Alex, look her over very carefully. I want to make sure she's sound before we try and make this trip with her."

"Yes, sir."

"And stop off and get Claude. I want him to see it, too. Billy, change places with Claude in the watch."

"Yes, sir, Colonel."

With Nanos's coast guard experience and Hayes's Navy background, Barrabas wanted them both to see the boat and then hear what they had to say.

"Okay, go now," he told them.

After Hatton, Nanos and Billy Two left, Barrabas phoned room service to order coffee for himself and O'Toole.

"I hope Lee did all right with the boat, Colonel," O'Toole said. "This is not going to be an easy trip."

"I'm sure she did fine, O'Toole." Actually Barrabas secretly wished he had been able to spare either Hayes or Nanos to come down to Key West and rent the boat. It had been a big responsibility to leave to Hatton, but he was sure she'd been up to it.

After the coffee arrived, Barrabas and O'Toole sat around and did some brainstorming.

"Colonel, if we're dealing with fifty inexperienced men, how do you intend to utilize them?"

"I haven't decided, Liam," Barrabas said. "We'll have to do some reconnaissance first, and see how well they respond to training. According to Jessup, we may not have to go up against the entire militia in order to oust Trieste."

"How's that?"

"He says Trieste has a death squad that he uses to keep the people in line. When someone gets out of line, they end up missing, or dead."

"That's his power, then," O'Toole summed up, and Barrabas nodded briefly in agreement.

"If we get rid of them, we get rid of him," O'Toole added.

"That's the way it seems," Barrabas said, "but first we'll have to identify them."

O'Toole shot a quizzical look at Barrabas. "And what about this Jules Berbick? You mentioned something about him not wanting to be president."

Barrabas grinned conspiratorially, then sobered. "Jessup feels he'll succumb and then live up to the responsibility, especially since President Trieste had his family murdered. Besides, we agreed to put him in office, not to stay and keep him there. What happens after we leave is not our business."

"Unless Jessup asks us to make it our business."

"Unless he *pays* us to make it our business."

"I guess this is all useless theorizing until we get there," O'Toole said.

"Let's go over the weapons we have," Barrabas suggested. "At least we can decide now how to dole them out."

"Why not?" O'Toole said. "It's something to do."

Barrabas was feeling the edginess that came from inactivity, just as O'Toole was, along with the others. The only time they'd felt alive over the past week was when they'd taken the weapons out of the warehouse that night, and that had only been a small taste of action.

Once they actually got on that boat, heading for Honduras, they'd all be able to taste the action in the air.

LEE HATTON HAD RENTED a car, and she drove Nanos and Hayes to the dock where the boat she'd acquired was kept.

She parked and got out of the car, saying, "This way."

They followed her to the end of the dock where it was tied. She merely said, "That's it."

Nanos and Hayes exchanged somewhat surprised glances. They were looking at a thirty-foot Challenger, completely rigged for sport fishing, with a fighting chair and an elevated steering station. It was much more than either of them had expected to see.

"How did you manage to get this with the money the colonel gave you?" Nanos asked.

"I made a down payment on the rental."

"A down payment?" Nanos echoed. "What down payment? The money he gave you was it."

"Well, nobody has to know that." She grinned. She was wearing a halter top and cutoff jeans and looked every inch a Florida sun bunny. Since much of their work was done outdoors, she even had the tan to match the look.

"Who's ripping who off?" Nanos asked.

"Oh, shut up and look it over."

BARRABAS WAS VERY PLEASED with his marine experts' reports on the boat.

"She's sound, Colonel," Nanos announced, and Hayes nodded his agreement. "Lee did a hell of a job getting the deal she did."

"We'll try to make sure they get it back," Barrabas said.

The only advantage they would have gleaned from doing an up-and-up business with Rivera and his people was they would have had a driver to take the boat back to Key West after they were dropped off.

"Colonel?" Hatton said.

"Yes, Lee?"

"Excuse me for asking," she went on, "but I've heard a lot of talk of how we're going to get to El Salvador. How are we going to get back?"

"Getting out empty-handed is not going to be nearly as hard as getting in with the weapons we have," Barrabas explained. "Actually, you may have given us the way out, though."

"How's that?"

"The boat," he said. "We can always come right back the way we came. Since we don't have a driver to bring the boat back, we can anchor it and hope to God it's still there when we are ready. That way, even the rental agency will be happy."

"That would be spiffy," Hayes said, "since the agency we got the van from is going to be pissed—when they find it, that is."

"All right, you people can go and get something to eat. Alex, I want you and Claude to make sure that boat is fueled up and ready to go tomorrow."

"Are we leaving tomorrow?" Nanos asked.

"Day after tomorrow," Barrabas said. It was almost dinnertime, and he wanted them to rest up from the drive. "Is there enough fuel aboard?"

"Yes, sir," Nanos said, "Lee took care of that, too."

Barrabas gave Lee Hatton an interested look.

"Research," she said. "There wasn't much else to do, so I researched how much fuel we'd need to make the trip, and bought it."

He nodded but said nothing.

In truth, Hatton had done much more research than she let on. Upon her arrival in Key West she had gone to the library and read what she could about deep-sea fishing. After that she had gone to several dealers and asked questions, as if she were shopping. Of course, it helped that she had worn halter tops and shorts and that her attractive appearance and friendly manner ensured the salesmen did not mind spending so much time with her. After such preliminary preparations she had finally made the rounds of the rental agencies and picked out an appropriate vessel.

"Alex," Barrabas said, "you and Claude take these maps. I want to make sure you both know the way."

"Yes, sir," Nanos replied, taking the rolled-up maps from Barrabas.

"Oh, and before you all leave, somebody give me the watch list on the van," the white-haired mercenary instructed, "so I know who's in it at all times."

"I'll need a list, too," Hatton said.

Nanos and Hayes left right away. O'Toole prepared the list for Barrabas and Hatton, and then he, too, stalked through the door.

Hatton was the last, and as she headed for the door, Barrabas called out. "Lee."

"Yes?"

"You did a fine job."

Hatton stared at him for a moment, not sure how to react. Barrabas rarely took special pains to give praise. A flash of silent appreciation in his eyes was more his usual style. Not that he withheld or begrudged praise, but only that he was a little sparing with it. That gave it far greater weight with his followers. Then she said, "Thank you, Colonel," and left.

Barrabas walked over to the window to look out over the crystal-blue water. Things had gone very smoothly to date, even with the impromptu nighttime raid they'd had to make to get the guns. They'd be leaving day after tomorrow, and that was when the mission would really start.

Barrabas was not superstitious, but the fact that all had gone well up to this point meant only one thing to him: if there was trouble it was ahead of them and not behind.

That was not where he liked trouble to be.

BARRABAS SPENT much of the next day in his room, preparing for what was to come once they reached Central America. He had to decide who would stay with Berbick and his people in the mountains, training them, and who would go with him to the capital, first on reconnaissance, and then to take the initial step toward engaging the new president's regime. Of course, final decisions would have to wait until they were actually there. For now he was simply treating it as an exercise.

While he was doing that, the other SOBs were running time down in their own ways, when they weren't on duty guarding the van.

Billy Two stayed in his room, trusting that he'd get a visit from Hawk Spirit.

Alex Nanos and Claude Hayes worked on the boat, getting it ready to go and enjoying every minute of it.

Liam O'Toole found some decent cigars and idled around in the hotel bar, and spent some time in his room reading.

Lee Hatton didn't want to stay in her room alone for fear that she'd spend most of the time thinking about Geoff Bishop, so she shopped, knowing that whatever she bought she'd have to leave behind, anyway. Still, the shopping was therapeutic, and nothing else. When she could shop no more she spent time watching Nanos and Hayes work on the boat.

All those varied activities did not take away the feeling of time, as though they were all willing the sand in a huge hourglass to flow faster. Or, as Barrabas thought when he stopped to stare out the window, as though a giant bowstring were pulled taut, and the arrow was on the verge of flight. Straight and true.

TRIESTE REGARDED the six men standing before his desk critically.

"If we have done something to displease you, *presidente*, please forgive us and tell us what it was."

Magnanimously President Trieste said, "You have not displeased me, Captain. On the contrary, you, my special president's squad, have comported yourself very well—except for one little thing."

"And that is?" Captain José Velez asked anxiously.

In a split second the magnanimous look on Trieste's face vanished, to be replaced by one of rage. "You have not yet found Berbick!" he shouted, slamming his fist on his desk. "You allowed him to escape, and you have not yet captured him."

"What danger can he be to you?" the captain asked.

"What danger?" Trieste echoed. "The people were not wholly in favor of Colon, but he was their recognized leader. Berbick was his vice president. I must be rid of him before the people will recognize me."

"The people revere you—"

"Do not be foolish!" Trieste shouted, again slamming his fist on the desk. "The people fear me!"

Next to Captain Velez stood Sergeant Roberto Barrio. He was the man who had actually pulled the trigger and killed President Colon. He looked now at President Trieste and knew that if it would serve his own purpose he'd pull the trigger on him also.

The people fear you? Barrio thought smugly. The people fear us, your special squad, the one they call a "death squad." But he did not say a word. Velez was the captain, let him deal with the president's criticisms.

"I have my regular patrols out looking for Berbick," Caesar Armande Trieste said. "But I am quite certain someone in town must be in contact with him. Someone who knows his hiding place—where he is preparing an insurrection against me!" He paused to scowl angrily. "I want you on their trail. Find them!"

"And kill them."

"Of course kill them, but after they tell you where Berbick is."

"Yes, sir."

"Now go!"

As they turned to leave, Trieste said, "Barrio, you stay."

Barrio turned and stood silently, looking at Trieste.

Before Trieste's ambition had turned him into the new president of El Salvador, he had been a teacher at the university. His subject had been history, and his passion had been military history. He felt eminently qualified to be president because he felt that he had learned from the mistakes of others.

"The other five, they are loyal to me," Trieste said to Barrio. "You, on the other hand, are loyal to yourself. If it suited your own purposes, you'd slit my throat in a minute, wouldn't you?"

Barrio held the president's gaze for a few moments, then answered, "Yes."

"Ah, good. Honesty. I appreciate that. You're the one who killed President Colon, aren't you?"

"Yes."

"Why?"

"Because by doing so I elevated my own position."

"Do you aspire to be a captain?"

"No."

"President?"

Barrio laughed and said, "No."

"Then what?"

"I'm not sure, Mr. President," Barrio said.

"When will you know?"

Barrio shrugged.

"How old are you?"

"Twenty-eight."

"Then you have a lot of time to decide," Trieste said. "I am forty-eight, and my time is shorter than yours. I have what I want now. If you help me to keep it, you will have what you want—when you decide what that is."

"What do you want me to do?"

"What I tell you to do, and at the time when I tell you," Trieste said, "and only because it will serve your own purpose."

Barrio hesitated a few moments, then said, "I think I can promise you that."

"You may go."

Barrio turned and left the office, and Trieste walked to his window and looked down at California Street. Every ruler who had ever depended on loyalty had been either killed or ousted. He planned to stay in office by depending on fear to silence any opposition, and by ambition. He'd build on others' fear, and on their driving ambition.

He wasn't sure how Barrio would help him, but realized that the man would not refuse when the time came. He would not refuse because there was no loyalty there to waver.

The man on whom Trieste would rely on was motivated only by self-interest, and that never failed.

JULES BERBICK SAT in the sun, enjoying the way it felt on his face. He wished that quiet pleasures like this would always be his only concern, but he knew that there were people within his country who wanted him to be president.

The call had come from without the country, too—from the United States.

Francisco Melendez had told him that assistance was coming, and it was of the kind that would do away with Trieste and get him, Berbick, in to succeed Colon.

The easiest way to overthrow a government was right from within its ranks, the way Trieste had done it. Berbick, however, had no one inside Trieste's government, and so would have to resort to force, the way the Contras had tried to go against Colon, and were now trying the same against Trieste. That was not an easy thing to accomplish.

Melendez had assured him that the mercenary force that was coming would be strong enough to put him into office.

Before he became vice president Berbick had been a rancher. Well, he called himself a rancher, but he had in truth been a farmer. He had also been Manuel Colon's friend, and so when Colon became president and asked him to be vice president, he had accepted.

That President Colon might come to harm, that he might die or be assassinated, was to have been expected. What Berbick had never expected was that his own family would be slaughtered, that he would end up on the run, hiding in the mountains, trying to stay alive so that he might someday become president.

He had never expected any of those things, and yet they had all come to pass—save the last one.

That one he did not want.

Trieste had ordered the murder of his family. For that he wanted to see Trieste dead—but he had to convince the world that he was not the man to replace him as president.

Maybe he would be able to convince the mercenaries of that, when they arrived.

ON THE MORNING of their departure, Barrabas and the others drove the van right onto the dock where the boat was and proceeded to load the guns on board.

With Hatton coordinating, they soon had all the crates stowed below, covered with blankets. Of course, that wouldn't keep the coast guard from finding the stuff if they were stopped, but there was no valid reason to fear that eventuality.

Still, as a good precaution, they covered the crates carefully.

"Billy, park the van," Barrabas instructed Billy Two. To Nanos he shouted, "Alex, start the engines!"

"Untie those lines!" Nanos in turn shouted to Hayes and O'Toole.

Billy Two parked the van and came running back as they were ready to get under way.

"Alex, let Claude take us out. Get some fishing gear ready and stick one of us in that seat so we'll look like we know what we're doing—just in case anyone's interested.''

"Billy, you're the biggest," Nanos said.

"What's that got to do with it?" Billy Two asked.

"Just in case we hook a whale..."

5

Francisco Melendez peered out through the darkness that covered the Gulf of Honduras. Had there been a full moon—or something more than the sliver that was hanging in the sky—he would have had better visibility.

In fact, he hadn't been able to see a damned thing for the past three nights, and he was starting to feel a chill in his bones from constantly sitting just off the beach, waiting for the American mercenaries' boat to arrive. It did get kind of cold when you were sitting by the ocean, even in June.

Francisco was beginning to worry about Jules Berbick. He was starting to think that maybe Berbick really didn't want to be president, after all. That is, Berbick had mentioned his lack of desire for the position on occasion, but it was only just recently that Francisco had begun to believe it. He was actually seeing it in Berbick's face. If it was true, then what were they fighting for—or preparing to fight for? President Colon was dead, and if Jules Berbick wasn't prepared to take up where he left off, then Colon's followers—his devoted followers—were lost.

Francisco's brother, Silvio, was in Orlando. He was the one who had contacted the United States government, and the one who was giving them whatever intelligence he could. Silvio had assured his brother that help was on the way.

It was Silvio who had Francisco sitting out here on the fringe of the beach for three nights in a row... waiting.

SILVIO MELENDEZ WAS OPENING the door to his apartment in Orlando when a driving fist from behind the door slammed into his chest. He staggered back, his legs working furiously and his arms windmilling as he tried to maintain his balance.

The man at the door hauled him inside and shut the door. He closed the distance between himself and the diminutive Salvadoran just as Silvio was regaining his balance.

The intruder slammed a fist into Silvio's stomach, doubling the smaller man over. He sank to the floor, retching, and the intruder stepped back quickly to avoid having his shoes splashed.

When Silvio finished emptying his stomach, the intruder put his hand on the back of his neck and held him in that position.

"I bring greetings from President Trieste," Roberto Barrio said, then pushed Silvio's face down into his own vomit.

"Please," Silvio said fearfully, "please!"

"Please what?" Barrio asked.

"D-do not kill me!"

"Ah," Barrio said, "but I will kill you, very slowly and painfully, unless you tell me exactly what I want to know. Do you hear?"

When Silvio didn't answer, Barrio shoved his face down into his vomit again, this time rubbing it back and forth.

"Yes, yes!" Silvio sobbed. "Yes, I hear you!"

"Bueno," Barrio said, "very good. We cooperate with each other, no?"

"If I tell you," Silvio asked, gasping for air as the vomit dropped from his face, "if I tell you, will you let me live?"

"Let you live?" Barrio asked. "No, no, that is not part of the deal. You see, the deal is you talk, and I will kill you quickly and painlessly. If you do not talk, you will die very slowly and very painfully."

To illustrate his point Barrio used his other hand to grasp the thumb of Silvio's right hand. He twisted it, bringing the entire arm up behind him, and then increased the pressure until the thumb cracked audibly.

Silvio screamed, and to drown out the sound Barrio pushed the man's face down into his vomit again.

He was lying, of course. Once Silvio talked—and for sure he would talk—Barrio intended to torture the little man to death.

Because he would enjoy it immensely.

ARMANDE TRIESTE was worried. Had he waited too long to send Barrio to the United States, to Orlando, Florida? If he had, then the information about the coming of the mercenaries would be too late. Possibly they had already arrived. Even if that were so, he continued to reason, at least he'd have some information on who they were and on their strength in numbers.

That would help to cut down their element of surprise, if nothing else.

Still, he wished he had decided on the move sooner.

WALKER JESSUP LOOKED down at the battered, mutilated body of Silvio Melendez. When the Salvadoran had not met him at the agreed-upon place, Jessup had decided to check it out. His thought was that perhaps the man had returned to El Salvador now that the SOBs were on their way.

For the Salvadoran's sake he wished in retrospect that the man had done exactly that.

ROBERTO BARRIO BOARDED his flight on time. He had been in Orlando for five hours, only long enough to locate Silvio Melendez and complete his business. Now he was returning to El Salvador with what little information Silvio had been able to supply him with.

It wasn't much, certainly not enough to satisfy President Trieste, but it would be more than what he'd had before.

The timing was off because Trieste should have sent him sooner, Barrio thought. That kind of hesitation, that kind of mistake, was not what he expected from someone with great leadership qualities.

Now, Roberto Barrio concluded, what does that say about our illustrious *presidente*. Surely there is a lesson there.

THE TRIP HADN'T BEEN uneventful. Negotiating the gulf had been no problem, although at one point, as they were approaching the Yucatán Channel, they had thought they were going to have to engage a government cutter from Cuba. Billy Two had hopped into the chair and, just by chance, had hooked a medium-size lemon shark. That had apparently satisfied the Cubans, who waved them on.

They got through the channel easily enough, between Cape Catoche, Mexico and Cape San Antonio, Cuba, passed Cancun and Cozumel and entered the

Caribbean. Honduras was due south from there, while due east were the Caymans and Jamaica.

Nanos did most of the piloting, with Hayes standing by to spell him. For a while Nanos had Lee Hatton with him in the pilothouse, showing her how to steer, but when they encountered a squall off Belize, Nanos had to take the wheel back from Lee. After that, Hatton refused to touch the wheel.

Barrabas was sitting in the chair, not fishing but just thinking when he heard the engine cut off.

"Colonel," he heard Nanos call immediately.

He turned in the chair, then got up and walked to where the Greek was standing. "What is it?"

"We're here. I assume you don't want to go into the gulf in daylight."

"No, we'll wait until dark," Barrabas said.

"How close are we going to get?"

"I'm assuming our man is smart enough to have a boat handy. We'll anchor her in deep water and leave her."

"And hope she's still here when we get back," Nanos said.

"Depending on the size of his boat, we may have to make a couple of trips to bring in these crates," Liam O'Toole put in.

"Then we'll make them," Barrabas said, checking his watch. They still had two hours before dark. "Get some rest," he told the others. "When we get ashore, we'll have a long trip ahead of us."

"I'm just glad this part of it is over," Lee Hatton said. She still hadn't fully recovered from their encounter with the squall and considered that it had probably ruined her for any future cruise plans.

IT WAS THE FOURTH NIGHT of waiting, and Francisco thought the vigil would start to seem unending when he suddenly noticed a light out in the gulf. He stood up, peering into the darkness, and then saw it once more, which confirmed his expectations. He hurried to his truck to get behind the wheel and give the signal with his headlights.

After that, he dashed to his outboard, pushed it into the water, hopped in and began rowing. He wouldn't use the engine until he was farther out.

At last, he thought jubilantly, at last they are here!

"I HEAR AN ENGINE, Colonel," Billy Two said.

Barrabas waited a few minutes, then said, "Yes, so do I."

The SOBs were dressed in fatigues now, their M-16s on their backs. The crates had been carted up from below, and they were sitting on them as they waited for their contact.

"Our ride's here, Colonel," O'Toole said as the outboard approached.

"From the size of that thing, we may have to make three trips," Nanos commented, "unless some of us want to swim."

"Let's make three trips," Lee Hatton said.

The outboard came alongside. The man in it tossed a rope to Billy Two, who then reached down and assisted him on board.

"*¡Madre de Dios!*" the man breathed.

"What's wrong?" Barrabas asked.

"*Uno, dos, tres...*" the man said, counting under his breath. "*Dios*, are there only four... four of you, and a woman? Five of you?"

"Oh no," Nanos said. "We're more than five."

"Ah, *gracias*—" the man began with obvious relief, and at that exact moment Claude Hayes appeared from below.

"There's six of us," Nanos said on cue, smiling so brightly his teeth shone in the dark.

"*¡Dios!*" the man exclaimed once more, his eyes betraying his horror.

"How many did you expect?" Barrabas asked him.

"I—I do not know, *señor*—"

"Then how can you be disappointed?" Barrabas asked. The man shrugged helplessly and Barrabas put a hand on his shoulder. "What is your name?" he asked him.

"Melendez, *señor*, Francisco Melendez."

"Can I call you Francisco?"

"*Sí, señor . . .*"

"Francisco, don't worry. We have more than enough people for what we have to do."

"Truly, *señor*?"

"Truly," Barrabas said, but the Salvadoran still looked dubious.

"We have supplies to take to shore, Francisco," Barrabas said. "So we should get started."

"*Sí, señor,*" the man answered obediently. "We will get started, just as you say."

THE TRUCK WAS an old flatbed whose sides had been built up with pieces of lumber that must have been scavenged from rotted huts and shacks. On the back of that truck was the poorest excuse for a corral that Barrabas had ever seen.

After three trips from the Challenger to shore, they loaded the crates onto the truck and lashed them down with rope supplied by Francisco. The rope, too, appeared to have been scavenged, and they wrapped it around two or three times to try to compensate for its poor condition.

Francisco was morose for the whole trip, so Barrabas sat up front with him and got him to talk.

The Salvadoran talked about how the Honduran government had forced the Nicaraguan refugees and the Miskitos to go back to their own country, where they'd have to fight for their lives every day instead of getting a breather once in a while by crossing into Honduras.

He talked about how El Salvador had been split into three factions ever since the death of Colon. There were Trieste and his people, Berbick and his small band of followers, and the Contras, who wanted neither Trieste nor Berbick in power.

"They were against Presidente Colon also. The fools did not see that he was the salvation of our country."

"And now that role falls to Jules Berbick?" Barrabas asked.

"Sí, señor."

"If he'll accept it."

Francisco looked at Barrabas in surprise and said, *"Sí, señor.* You know, then, that Jules is showing no interest in being president?"

"I've heard rumors to that effect."

The roads that they were traveling were in poor condition, and Barrabas asked when they would reach the main road.

"Señor," Francisco replied, "this *is* the main road." The little bandy-legged Salvadoran laughed for the first time since Barrabas had met him. "Wait, *señor* until we have to take the supply roads."

Francisco explained that instead of taking a direct route to the Salvadoran border he had mapped out a route that, if all went well, would keep them out of contact with the Honduran army patrols.

"They would not take kindly to our carrying weapons through their country."

"I should think not," Barrabas said, and they continued on in silence.

On a decent Florida highway a hundred miles would have taken them less than two hours. After two hours in Francisco's rickety old truck, they hadn't even covered half that distance.

Barrabas watched with interest as the muscles in the little Salvadoran's arms bunched and clenched as he wrestled the truck through main road and supply roads, but Barrabas could barely tell the difference. Never again would he refer to a hole in an American highway as a pothole, not after some of the holes Francisco had managed to miss.

As rough as the ride was for Barrabas in the cab, he knew that the others had it even rougher in the back of the truck, trying to keep the gun crates from breaking free while making sure they didn't fall off.

At one point steam began to rise from beneath the hood, and Francisco stopped the truck at the side of the road. "We must quench her thirst and wait a short while, *señor*," he said. He grabbed a plastic container of water from behind his seat and got out.

Barrabas stepped out on his side and walked to the back of the truck as Lee Hatton dropped from the flatbed.

"Ooh," she said, rubbing her behind and lower back, "I've got bruises where I never knew I could have bruises."

Nanos and O'Toole jumped down while Billy Two and Hayes checked the crates.

"Alex, you and Billy have a look around."

"Yes, sir."

Billy, too, got down from the truck. He went off to one side of the road while Nanos checked the other side and O'Toole climbed up to help Hayes.

"How far are we from the border, Colonel?" Lee Hatton asked. She had taken a handkerchief from the pocket of her fatigues and was mopping the sweat from her face and neck.

"According to Francisco we're a little more than halfway there."

"How fast has he been going?"

"I don't think this crate can do more than thirty."

"Seems like more when you're riding back here," she said, but she wasn't hinting that he change places with her. In fact, the thought had never occurred to either of them. Whatever they had to do, she did her part just like the others.

"*¿Señor?*" Francisco said, coming behind him.

"Yes, Francisco?"

"We can move on now, *señor*."

"In a minute."

"*Sí, señor.*"

After three minutes Nanos appeared, and a half a minute later Billy Two returned.

"All right," Barrabas said. "Let's mount up."

As they continued on Barrabas asked Francisco about the Berbick supporters.

"We are all in the mountains, *señor*," Francisco said. "We are devoted to putting Jules Berbick into the presidential palace to continue the work begun by Presidente Colon."

If only Berbick were as devoted to the same thing, Barrabas thought.

Francisco went on to tell Barrabas what fighters his people were. All they needed, he said, was someone to arm them properly and show them the way. They were ready, he said, to charge right into the capital.

"Straight to their deaths," Barrabas said.

"If necessary, *señor*," Francisco said, puffing out his chest. "We are not afraid to die."

"I am not afraid to die either, Francisco," Barrabas said, "but I am afraid to die stupidly."

"How do you mean that, *señor*?"

"You haven't the force to even consider marching into the capital."

"How else can we—"

"Leave the how else to me and my people, Francisco," Barrabas said. "That's what we're here for."

That served to remind Francisco of the small numbers of the force commanded by Barrabas. What, he asked, could six people hope to do?

"It is not how many we are," Barrabas said, "but how much damage we can do."

Francisco whipped the wheel to the left to avoid a craterlike opening in the road and shook his head, either at the hole or at what Barrabas had just said. The merc warrior did not know which, and did not ask for clarification.

Suddenly, as they turned a corner, they saw a jeep on the road ahead. Francisco reacted instantly by slamming on the brakes and shifting into reverse. When they had backed out of sight around the bend, he stopped.

"*¡Soldados!*" he said.

"Looking for us?" Barrabas asked.

"I do not think so," Francisco said. "How could they know?"

"Would the Hondurans cooperate with Trieste?"

"If he told them about the guns, perhaps."

"Colonel?" O'Toole asked, appearing at the window.

"Soldiers."

"I saw them," O'Toole said, "but I don't think they saw us."

"Maybe not," Barrabas said. "They'd probably be on us by now if they had."

"What do we do?" O'Toole asked.

"We take them," Barrabas said, "but I don't want them killed. The last thing we need is to announce our arrival with a firefight." Barrabas looked at Francisco and asked, "How many did you see?"

"Four," the Salvadoran answered without hesitation.

The man had good eyes. Barrabas had also counted four, and O'Toole chimed in his agreement.

"All right," Barrabas said, "get out and hit them from both sides. I'll stay in the truck. That should draw at least one of them to me."

"Yes, sir."

"And remember, no shooting, and don't kill any of them if you don't have to."

"Gotcha."

O'Toole went to the back and pulled the others off the truck, and they melted into the jungle on either side. Barrabas gave them enough time to get situated before giving Francisco the go-ahead. When the Salvadoran didn't start the truck right away, Barrabas turned his head to carefully check him out. He was biting his lip, and the old .45 in his lap was held in hands that were none too steady.

"Francisco," Barrabas said. "We have to move."

"Huh?" The little man had a glazed look in his eyes.

The merc leader reached over and took the gun out of Francisco's trembling hands.

"Leave this part to us, amigo," he said. "All you have to do is drive. *¿Comprendes?*"

Francisco squinted at Barrabas and nodded his head. *"Sí, señor. Comprendo."*

"All right," Barrabas said and held the .45 in his own lap. "Drive...slowly."

Francisco started the engine and started the truck moving at a crawl toward the jeep.

"When he tells you to stop, do it," Barrabas said. "We'll take care of the rest."

"S-sí, señor."

As they approached they noted that there were two sitting in the jeep and two out. One of the standing ones looked up and tapped the other on the shoulder. That soldier said something, and the other two in the jeep looked up.

"Here we go," Barrabas said.

One of the soldiers outside the jeep started walking toward the truck. After he'd gone five feet, the second one followed suit. It was a smart move for them not to walk together; the tactic kept enough room between them so they both couldn't be taken out by one man.

But one of them would reach the truck first and Barrabas had decided he would handle that situation. The other he would have to leave up to somebody else.

As the soldier drew closer to the truck, he was moving in on Francisco's side. Barrabas had expected that and was glad he'd taken the gun away from the Salvadoran.

The soldier walked up to Francisco's window and spoke something in rapid-fire Spanish, but before

Francisco could attempt to answer, Barrabas got his attention by calling out, *"¿Señor?"*

The man leaned over to look past Francisco at Barrabas, and the SOB leader drew closer to the window and stuck the .45 in the soldier's face.

"Tell him not to move," Barrabas said to Francisco, who in turn relayed the message to the soldier. The soldier obeyed with a frightened look on his face.

The other soldier, who had been following about five feet behind, saw that something was wrong. He instinctively reached for the AK-47 that was slung on his back. Before he could bring it around, Billy Two appeared behind him and clubbed him over the back of the head.

Up by the jeep the two soldiers saw what was happening and leaped down. Before they could move, O'Toole, Nanos, Hayes and Hatton emerged from the jungle at both sides of the road, and they raised their hands at the sight of the guns bristling in their direction.

Billy Two came over to the truck and relieved the soldier of his weapons. Only then did Barrabas exit from the truck.

"All right," he said to the Osage, "take him back to the jeep. Let's get them off the road."

They tied all four soldiers up and dumped them into the jeep, which Claude Hayes had driven off the road and into the jungle.

"They're tied good and tight, Colonel," he said. "They won't be loose for a long time, unless somebody finds them."

"If they're the patrol for this area, there won't be another until they're missed. By that time we should be in El Salvador."

Liam O'Toole stood scratching his head with an uncertain look on his face. He was taking small steps as though he were trying to stomp around in a circle while he was deciding whether he should speak up.

"I know, Liam," Barrabas said, "but we've got to take this chance. Let's get moving."

6

The truck stopped, and Barrabas looked at Francisco.

"Why are we stopping?"

"Señor," he said, "from here we walk."

Away from the threatening confrontation with the soldiers—which had taken place hours ago—Francisco was once again calm and efficient, if still somewhat morose.

Barrabas got out of the truck and shouted, "All right, everybody off."

"Is this it, Colonel?" O'Toole asked.

"From here we walk."

"Carrying these crates?"

"Francisco!" Barrabas shouted.

"¿Sí, señor?"

"We were to have help."

"Sí, señor," Francisco said. "The Miskitos. They will be here in the morning."

"The morning?"

"Sí, señor. We cannot travel through the jungle at night. The swamps are hard to negotiate, even by day. By night they are treacherous."

Barrabas didn't like that. Staying in one place all night was dangerous, especially if the soldiers they'd tied up were found. Barrabas knew that what O'Toole had left unsaid back there was true. Killing those soldiers would have increased their insurance, but he'd made his decision and now had to deal with the situation the best he could.

"All right," Barrabas said, "let's set up a watch schedule."

"Should we unload the crates, Colonel?" O'Toole asked.

"No," Barrabas said. "Let's do that in the morning, when the Indians get here."

To be on the safe side, they set up their schedule so that two of them would be awake at all times.

"One stays with the truck, and one moves around," Barrabas instructed. "If trouble is coming, I want to know before it gets here. If it does sneak up on us, I don't want it getting to those guns."

Nanos and Hayes took the first watch, O'Toole and Billy Two the second and Barrabas and Hatton the third. Barrabas told Francisco to get a good night's sleep, because he was their guide.

They made camp off the road. Francisco slept in the cab of the truck while the others, bedded down on the ground in sleeping bags provided by Francisco.

Barrabas didn't sleep well and was already awake when O'Toole shook him.

"Wake Hatton," Barrabas said.

"Yes, sir."

Barrabas wanted to give Billy Two his sleeping bag, but the big Osage declined.

"I've slept enough, Colonel," he said. "I'd like to move around a bit, maybe scout ahead."

"Be careful of the swamps," Barrabas warned.

"I've been in swamps before, Colonel."

"All right," Barrabas said, "but don't stay away too long."

"I'll be back before first light."

"Colonel?" Hatton came up on him after Billy Two had disappeared into the jungle.

"Lee, you take the truck."

"Where's Billy going?"

Barrabas looked at her and said, "Probably to commune with Hawk Spirit, unless I miss my guess."

They exchanged a faint smile and resumed their respective duties.

The night passed uneventfully, and in the morning Billy Two returned with six Miskito Indians.

"Ran into them and thought I'd bring them back. They didn't seem to be in a real hurry to get here."

"Miskitos don't mind fighting," Francisco said, "but they are not used to the idea of routine work."

"How'd you get them to agree to come and help?" Barrabas asked.

Francisco smiled. "I told them you'd pay them."

"You did, huh?" Barrabas said.

"Was that all right?"

"Yeah, Francisco," said Barrabas, "that was fine. Come on, let's get the truck unloaded."

They were already putting their backs to the job when O'Toole stopped them. "Wait a minute," he said in a puzzled tone.

"What's wrong?" Barrabas asked.

"There should be four crates, Colonel," O'Toole said. "Don't know why I didn't notice it before, but there's five here."

Barrabas looked at the four crates on the ground, and then at the fifth on the truck. It wasn't as long as the other four.

"Who put that crate on the van back in Florida?" Barrabas asked.

"I did," Nanos confessed.

"Why, Alex? What's in it?"

"Just something I thought we might be able to use."

"You going to make us guess?" O'Toole asked.

"Nah," Nanos said. He leaped up on the truck and pried open the crate with a knife. "Fragmentation grenades," he said, showing them one.

"Fragmentation grenades?" O'Toole repeated incredulously. "We've been carrying explosives for more than a thousand miles, and you didn't tell us?"

"Well, Liam," Nanos said, nudging O'Toole in the ribs, "I wanted to surprise you. Besides, I know how nervous you get around explosives."

The joke there was that Liam O'Toole, former army captain and IRA vet, was the group's explosives expert.

"You silly son of a bitch," O'Toole muttered.

"All right," Barrabas said, "unload it and let's get moving. They may come in handy, after all."

ARMANDE TRIESTE SAT BACK in his chair and looked through half-closed eyes at the captain of his private death squad.

"The news is not good, sir."

Trieste shut his eyes completely and waited.

"The mercenaries were stopped only once in Honduras, and they escaped."

"How many did they kill?"

"They did not kill any," the captain said. "They subdued four Honduran soldiers, tied them up and left them their jeep, which was then pushed off the road. The soldiers were not found until the next morning."

"Typical," Trieste said. "They are in El Salvador, by now, then."

"Probably."

"Do we know how many there were?"

"The soldiers said there were dozens."

"Covering for themselves, no doubt."

"Yes, sir."

"All right," Trieste said, "that's all, Captain."

"Thank you, sir."

The captain turned and left. Trieste folded his hands over his stomach and thought about what Roberto Barrio had told him when he'd returned from Orlando.

Silvio Melendez had been unable to provide an accurate count of the mercenaries, no matter how much Barrio had tortured him. Sending Barrio to Orlando had accomplished only one thing. They had made sure that Silvio Melendez would never again oppose President Trieste.

That was not enough, though. Trieste, who was angry at himself more than anyone else, insisted on holding on to the slightest edge, and at the moment that consisted of his knowledge that there were mercenaries in his country.

It was not much, but it was better than nothing, he consoled himself.

EL SALVADOR IS mostly mountainous, and thick jungles and roaring rivers offer the only relief from craggy peaks and steep, narrow valleys. The terrain was constantly pitching either man or vehicle up or down, and then up and down again. The jungle was dense, the swamps were hungry, and most rivers were powerful, usually flowing fast.

Over the next eight hours the Soldiers of Barrabas covered barely forty klicks. The Miskitos were strong and had good stamina, but even they needed to rest every so often while carrying the heavy gun crates, two to a crate.

To try to speed things up Barrabas had the SOBs switch off with the Indians the next day, to allow them to take a break from their load and still have the group maintaining a steady pace. The only one who was spared carrying the load was Hatton, and not because of her "femininity" but as a result of the simple fact that she just wasn't physically strong enough.

Even Francisco helped out. He was slightly built, but as Barrabas had observed in the truck, he was strong.

Hatton made herself valuable by going ahead to scout regularly with one of the other SOBs.

At noon the next day, when they'd resumed their march after a brief break from the humid, suffocating heat, Francisco made the announcement they'd all been waiting for.

"We are in El Salvador, *señors*," he said. "Welcome to my country."

JULES BERBICK WAS THE FIRST to see their approach. Six Miskitos carrying crates, and six mercenaries. He also spotted Francisco Melendez bringing up the rear.

Berbick shook his head. Six mercenaries? Was this the help Francisco had promised him?

Someone among Berbick's followers also noticed the arrival and raised the alarm. People emerged from their tents and waited while the newcomers climbed the rest of the slope to join them.

Hernando Paz had been in command during Francisco's absence, and he was the first to greet the mercenaries as they entered camp.

"Welcome, welcome!" he cried out, and behind him the rest of the rebels raised a cheer.

Francisco had freed himself from his load and shook hands with Hernando.

"I knew you would return," Hernando said to his friend, pumping his hand enthusiastically. He looked beyond Francisco at Barrabas and the SOBs, and then past them with a searching glance.

He frowned, then asked, "Where are the rest of them?"

"This is all there is, Hernando," Francisco said.

"All?" Hernando looked at them and counted out loud, but before he could object, Francisco cut him off.

"I have seen them," Francisco said. "They are very good, believe me."

"But six—"

"Is there someplace we can put our supplies?" Barrabas asked, stepping forward.

"Of course," Francisco said. He looked at Hernando and said, "Have someone show them to their quarters. We will talk later."

"*Sí,*" the other man said, "we will talk." He looked at Barrabas and said, "Come, I will show you myself."

The Miskitos picked up the four crates, and Hayes and Billy Two took the one holding the claymores. They all followed Hernando. He led them to what was easily the largest tent on the grounds.

"You will stay here," Hernando said. "Anything you need will be brought to you."

"We could use food and water," Barrabas said.

"*Sí, señor.* I will have it taken care of."

After Hernando left, Barrabas had the Miskitos deposit the crates inside the tent. When he'd paid them for their services, he entered.

The others were all waiting for him and now gathered around for a quick rundown of the next scenarios.

"All right, people," Barrabas said. "Listen up. We'll eat and rest briefly, then I'll want to take a look at what we have to work with here. After that, I'll hand out your assignments. Basically, some of you will stay here and train these people as well as you can, while the others will come with me on recon. We need some intel, and I want to get it as soon as possible."

"Colonel, how long do we have to train them?" O'Toole asked.

"I don't know, Liam," Barrabas answered. "I guess that depends on what kind of intelligence we get. We'll know more when I get back in a couple of days or so."

Actually, Barrabas didn't know how long he'd be gone because he didn't know how far they were from the capital. He'd have to find that out from Francisco and his people. Also, he wanted to meet Jules Berbick as soon as possible. If the man was adamant about not serving as president, there was really no point in going through all the trouble. If that was the case, then the only part of their mission left to fulfill would be to depose President Trieste and send him fleeing. That would actually be easier if they didn't have to deal with putting Berbick in office, and training his supporters.

At that point three women appeared with food and drink, and at their silent insistence the SOBs allowed themselves to be served. The meal consisted of some sort of well-done meat, as well as vegetables and fruit, followed by water as their drink.

Barrabas studied the women and wondered if they would be among the people to be trained. Two of them were sturdily built females in their late thirties, but the third was a lovely young woman in her twenties. The merc leader noticed that she had seen Nanos, and that Nanos had very much noticed her, and the quick exchange of glances indicated they both seemed to like what they were seeing.

"All right," Barrabas told the women, "we thank you. *Gracias*. You can leave now. *¡Vámanos!*"

They finally got the message and left the tent.

"Colonel, you think there are women among the rebels?" O'Toole asked.

"Come on, O'Toole!" Nanos said. "What do you think those were?"

"I meant as fighters, Nanos," O'Toole returned.

"Well, why not?" Barrabas asked. "We have a woman in our ranks, don't we? If there are women, I suppose we'll have to leave some of their training to Hatton."

Hatton simply nodded.

"What about Berbick?" O'Toole asked. "When do we meet him?"

"After we finish eating, I'll find Francisco or Hernando and see if we can't get that out of the way first. I'll talk to him first, and then the rest of you can have a turn."

"And if he still doesn't want to be president?" Hayes asked. "What do we do then?"

"We'll cross that bridge when we come to it," Barrabas said. "Let's eat. For those of us going on recon, this may be our last hot meal for a while."

They concentrated on their food with gusto, and after he'd finished, Barrabas picked himself up and went in search of Francisco. Along the way he passed groups of rebels, who all smiled in greeting, while some patted him approvingly on the back. They seemed to feel that he and the SOBs were going to be their saviors.

That remained to be seen.

He found Francisco in a small tent, sitting with Hernando. They were in a deep and animated discussion and stopped short when he appeared.

"I don't want to interrupt."

"You are not interrupting," Francisco assured him. "What can we do for you, Colonel?"

"I'd like to meet Vice President Berbick."

"Ah, of course. He will be expecting us." Francisco rose and said, "Come, I will take you to him."

Barrabas nodded to Hernando, who responded in kind, although he did not look like a happy man. The warrior followed Francisco back through the camp, again running the gauntlet of gratitude from the rebels.

"Francisco," Barrabas said, "I can't help but notice that you have some women in camp."

"Sí, señor."

"Will they also be training to fight?"

"But of course. That is why they are here. Oh, they do the cooking and mending, but all but a few of them will want to train with the weapons you have brought."

Barrabas didn't wonder at that. From what he had seen, those rebels who were armed were carrying ancient Chinese Type 56 assault rifles, and some Yugoslav M-70s.

Francisco led Barrabas to another tent. It was large, but not nearly as large as the one the SOBs were using.

"El Presidente?" Francisco said at the entrance.

A moment later the flap was thrown back, and Jules Berbick stepped out.

For a moment Barrabas was thrown off balance. He had not expected the man to be almost as big as Billy Two. Berbick was easily six foot five and would go at

240 if he was a pound. His skin was a caramel color, smooth, shiny and unblemished.

"*El Presidente*, this is Colonel Barrabas. He is the leader of the mercenaries."

Berbick stared at Barrabas for a moment with brown eyes that Barrabas could only describe as gentle. When Berbick extended his hand, Barrabas took it, half expecting a bone-crushing grip. What he got was a brief acquaintance with a soft, smooth-skinned hand that had not seen hard work recently for sure.

As if he had read the mercenary's mind, Berbick looked at his hand and said, "Once my hands were as calloused as yours, *señor*."

"I'm sure they were, sir."

"Please, come inside and we can talk."

Berbick held back the flap and Barrabas entered ahead of him. The two men were alone inside, because Francisco had left, having accomplished his job.

A cot was in a corner, and a small wooden table and two folding chairs were placed near the center of the tent.

"Please, sit," Berbick invited.

Barrabas sat and stared across the table at the huge man. As large as Berbick was, he seemed to Barrabas to be the epitome of the gentle giant.

"So, you have come to make me president, eh?" His attitude seemed to be one of bemusement.

"That's part of the plan, sir," Barrabas said. "Of course, that depends on you."

"On me," Berbick repeated. "Yes, on me." He stood up then and paced about. "These people," he said with a sweep of his arm to include everyone in camp, "they all seem to feel I am the man for the job."

"Yes, sir," Barrabas said, "that's what I've heard."

"Do you think I am the man for the job?"

"I don't have enough information to make a judgment like that."

"But your government does, eh?"

"I cannot speak for my government."

"But you are here on their behalf, are you not?"

"Excuse me, sir," Barrabas said, "but we are here on your behalf, and on behalf of your people."

"Yes, my people," Berbick said. "That is why I will permit you to put me in office, Colonel, in spite of the fact that I seem to be the only one who thinks I am not the man for the job."

"Why take it then?"

Berbick studied Barrabas for a long moment. "I gather you would not," Berbick said.

"No sir, not if I didn't want it."

"No," Berbick said, "no, I don't suppose you would. I, however, feel a responsibility."

"You have a responsibility to yourself also," Barrabas said, "just as I have to myself."

"Are you a selfish man, Colonel?"

"Sometimes," Barrabas said, "very often, probably."

"Then you are here for selfish reasons?"

Barrabas paused for a moment, searching for the right words. "I am here for self-serving reasons, but from what I understand, I'll be supporting a right cause."

"Well," Berbick responded, "I suppose my mission is to listen to my people's need and let you put me into office, sir."

"Yes, sir."

"I suppose we'll all see what happens after that, eh?"

Barrabas nodded silently and felt the respect strong men experience when they meet another strong man.

"I appreciate your presence, Colonel," Berbick said, "and the presence of your men—excuse me, your people. I noticed that you have a woman in your ranks."

"Yes, sir."

"Please relay to them my appreciation."

"I will, sir."

"I suppose you'll want to see what you have to work with here?"

"Yes, sir."

"Very well. Francisco and Hernando will introduce you to them all. They are good people, Colonel. All of them. Too good, I think, to die for me, but I cannot convince them of that."

"I suppose they think that if they do die, it will be for their country."

"Yes," Berbick said, "I'm sure that is what they think, Colonel."

Barrabas stood up, and Berbick followed suit. "Please," Berbick said, "you will call me Jules, eh? I am afraid I am somewhat between positions at the moment. I suppose you'll want some information about the president's residence and offices?"

"Yes, sir."

"Come back when it suits you, Colonel, and we will talk."

Berbick extended his hand and the two men shook, then Barrabas went in search of Francisco.

Barrabas arranged with Francisco to have the rebels line up so the SOBs could inspect them.

The first thing Barrabas wanted to do was weed out the rebels who were less than able-bodied. They wouldn't last through training, let alone in a firefight.

He counted a total of sixty-three, but by the time he'd pulled out the ones who were too young, too old or too sick, they were down to fifty-two. Seven of those were women. He assured the people whom he'd eliminated that they would still serve in some tangible way.

Once they had their potential army, Barrabas had O'Toole, Nanos and Hayes arm them, taking their weapons and passing out the AK-74s, the Berettas and the ammo belts. There were fifty AK-74s, so he had O'Toole give Francisco and Hernando each an M-16, like the ones the SOBs were carrying.

Barrabas left it to O'Toole to familiarize them with their weapons. Hatton was assigned to work with the Irishman, and particularly with the women.

While the other SOBs stood by and watched, Barrabas took Francisco and Hernando aside into their tent, showed them how to use the M-16s and Berettas and then talked to them about the capital.

As it turned out, they were a healthy day's hike from San Salvador, which surprised him.

"That seems awfully near."

Francisco and Hernando exchanged satisfied looks. "We thought that it was so close the militia would never suspect we were here. Besides, you really can't see us until you get real close."

Barrabas had noticed that. Once they had ascended to the peak of the mountain, he'd found that the camp was set up in what seemed to be a natural depression. It was spread out so that it would be difficult to spot even from the air. In fact, they had done quite well in choosing a campsite.

"Tomorrow I'll be taking most of my people to the capital. I want to get a look at things for myself, but I'd appreciate it if you could tell me what you know about their patrols."

"*Sí, señor,*" Francisco said. "As far as we know, they have regular patrols...."

NEXT DAY BARRABAS, Nanos, Billy Two and Hayes got an early start for their trek through the jungle to the capital, San Salvador. Francisco and one Miskito accompanied them to show the way, and just to make things faster, but on future trips the SOBs wouldn't need guides. Liam O'Toole and Lee Hatton stayed behind to begin the training program, which was an obvious priority.

The hike to San Salvador was roughly fifty-one klicks, and they made it in just under nine hours. Francisco and the Miskito led the way, cutting through the undergrowth with machetes.

When they stopped once to rest, Barrabas saw the Miskito looking into a bag that he must have had hidden on his body.

"What's in the bag, Francisco?"

Francisco looked, then looked away. "Do not look, Colonel. All of the Miskito carry that bag. It is made of—what do you call the thing that comes after the baby?"

"Placenta?"

"That is it, the placenta. Inside they keep a rock and a bird's nest."

"What does that mean?"

Francisco shrugged. "All I know is that they feel as long as the bag hangs around their body, they cannot be harmed by an enemy."

"From what I hear about the Miskitos who are fighting with the Contras, that's not necessarily the case."

"It is an old belief, Colonel," Francisco said, "the kind that dies hard."

When they continued, they waded through rushing rivers and waist-deep swamps. It was a good thing that the SOBs wore two or three pairs of heavy socks inside their boots, a habit they had picked up serving in Nam. In infantry, a soldier's most important possessions were his feet.

It was to their advantage currently that there were only six of them. Billy Two, walking the point, was able to warn them whenever a patrol was ahead. They could conceal themselves in time and effectively, and avoid a confrontation before they were ready.

Their vantage point in the jungle allowed them to take note of patrols coming and going from the city. What Francisco had told Barrabas was apparently correct. The patrols went out on a regular basis, usually twenty to twenty-five men in each. Their purposes were not always readily evident, and Barrabas decided that they'd stay the next day and watch carefully, trying to determine some sort of a pattern, and the reason for it.

They found a place to camp about five klicks out from the city, just to be on the safe side, and stood watch in twos. When the morning came around, Barrabas was up and alert. He and Billy Two woke the others, and they went back to the perimeter of the city.

They stayed all day, timing patrols. In one instance Barrabas had Billy Two tail a patrol.

When he returned he reported. "Colonel, they just seemed to be performing a circuit around the city. I don't think they're looking for anybody or anything in particular."

"Francisco, there's a lot of activity going on, lots of comings and goings. That doesn't sound normal, from what you told me."

"It is not, *señor*," Francisco said. "It is odd. I can't explain it . . . unless . . ."

"Yes, I know," Barrabas said, "unless they know we're here."

"They might know that *somebody* is here, Colonel," Hayes offered. "They could figure that out from what we did to those soldiers in the jeep."

"If that is the case," Francisco said, alarmed, "then they know how many of you there are—or how few."

"Not necessarily," Barrabas said.

"But Colonel, once those men report—"

"Nanos, if you were them, what would you report?"

Nanos smiled and said, "I'd lie, sir. I'd tell my CO that we were taken by a whole battalion."

"You see?" Barrabas said to Francisco. "No, I don't think they know how many—or as you say, how few—we are."

"But they know that somebody is here!" Francisco said.

"That's true," Barrabas said, "and all that means is that we don't have as much of an edge as we thought."

"What are we going to do, Colonel?" Hayes asked.

"Billy, can you get us back to the camp?"

"Sure, Colonel."

"All right," Barrabas said, turning to Francisco. "Francisco, take the Miskito and go back to camp. Tell Captain O'Toole that we're going to stir things up a little and will return about a day after you. Understand?''

''No, *señor*,'' Francisco said, looking puzzled. ''What is 'stir up'?''

''You know,'' Nanos explained, making motions with his hands, ''like when you stir a salad?''

''You are going to make the soldiers a salad?'' he asked, looking even more puzzled. Finally he shrugged and said, ''Ah well, I will give Captain O'Toole the message. Undoubtedly he will know what it means.''

''He'll know, Francisco,'' Barrabas said. ''Don't worry. Get going now.''

''You must be careful, Colonel,'' Francisco suggested with a shake of his head. ''We would not like to lose you so soon after your arrival.''

''We're not here to be careful, Francisco,'' Barrabas said, ''we're here to be effective—but we will take caution not to lose our heads.''

''I suppose that will have to do, *señor*,'' Francisco said. He shook hands with Barrabas and said, ''May the hand of God be with you, *señor*.''

''*Gracias*,'' Barrabas said. ''We could probably use one more hand.''

WHEN CAPTAIN VELEZ ENTERED President Trieste's office, he wondered if he was again going to get a severe dressing down. He was pleased to see that Captain Rodriguez of the regular militia was also there. The two captains did not like each other, and maybe it was Rodriguez who was going to have his own head handed to him.

''Velez!'' Trieste said. ''I want you to hear this.''

"Yes, sir."

Now Trieste spoke to Rodriguez. "Captain, I want to make a change in the schedule of the patrols."

"Yes, *presidente*. Uh, what kind of changes?"

"We have a band of mercenaries in our country, and I am expecting them to engage one of our patrols," Trieste said.

"Why would they do this, *presidente*?" Rodriguez asked, displaying his typical density.

Trieste frowned and said, "It will certainly be the way they will announce their arrival, Captain, and their intentions."

"Of course, *mi presidente*," Rodriguez said, trying to save face. "I knew that. Er, what would you have me do, then? Double the guard around the building?"

"No," Trieste said, with a look at Captain Velez, "I have my own people for that particular task. What I want you to do, Captain, is to send out backup patrols."

"Backup patrols," Rodriguez said. "Yes, sir."

"I want the initial patrols to be cut from twenty-five men to twenty, and then I want a second patrol sent out fifteen minutes behind them—"

"Yes, sir, as you—"

"Let me finish, Captain!"

"Of course, sir. I did not mean—uh, of course, please finish."

Glaring at the man and promising to have him replaced as soon as possible, Trieste continued. "I want the second patrol to be full strength, twenty-five men. If these mercenaries are counting on attacking twenty men, then they will find themselves facing a force of more than twice that size.''

"They will be taken by surprise," Rodriguez said.

"That is exactly right, Captain," Trieste agreed, with relish. "They will be surprised to death!"

7

A drop of perspiration rolled over the bridge of Nile Barrabas's nose, dangled from the tip and then fell and smashed itself against the corner of his right boot. It was a result of the intense heat, not nerves. Never nerves.

Barrabas didn't notice. Perspiration was the least of his worries as he stood stock-still in a Central American jungle, listening intently. He wore a headband to handle most of the sweat that would begin at his hairline, but every so often a drop would still slide down his face and fall from his nose or his chin. The only attention he paid to the drops was to rub their polka-dot pattern out of the dirt with his boot before he moved on. He knew from personal experience that signs of your bodily functions could give you away once you had moved on. If you didn't rub them out—or bury them— then you might as well have left a street sign, like a one-way arrow pointing in the direction you were moving.

Behind him he knew that three of his soldiers, Claude Hayes, Alex Nanos and Billy Two, were also listening intently. Liam O'Toole and Lee Hatton remained in the mountains with Berbick's people, trying their level best to whip them into some sort of shape for an attack on the capital. O'Toole was ideally suited to that kind of training, because no one knew weapons and explosives the way he did, and he was second only to Barrabas himself as far as tactics went.

Listening for the approach of soldiers from the capital, Barrabas couldn't help but think that they were engaged in one of the crazier of Walker Jessup's schemes, pitting the SOBs against the entire force of president Trieste's army. Granted, in a country the size of El Salvador that force was not monumental, but when you numbered only six almost any force was larger. And to have to face that army with only a rag-tag group of Berbick's supporters was crazier yet.

Still, Barrabas had accepted the job, so who was the crazier of the two after all, he or Jessup?

A sound from the jungle drew his attention. He lifted his head like an animal that sniffs the air looking for either prey or foe. If he had heard the sound, then the big Osage, Billy Starfoot, had heard it for sure.

Barrabas shifted his hands on his submachine gun. He was glad that they had decided to go with the more dependable, familiar M-16. He himself liked the newer Beretta AR-70s, and had been surprised that the guns had been available to them. Still, the AR-70s had not caught on in many places other than Jordan and Malaysia and had not been severely tested. Barrabas wouldn't have minded having one for himself, but in the end he had decided that the M-16 would be the weapon for this mission.

He felt Billy Two come up alongside him.

"They're coming, Colonel."

"I hear them," Barrabas said to the big Osage. "How many?"

"Twenty or more, I'd guess."

"Could be worse," Barrabas said.

Billy Two smiled. "It could always be worse, couldn't it, Colonel."

"I guess so. Take Alex and get into position, Billy."

"Yes, sir."

Barrabas would remain where he was, with Claude Hayes, while Alex "the Greek" and Billy Two crossed over to the other side of the trail. When the soldiers came into view, the four SOBs would fire at them diagonally. The terrain was too flat to set up an effective cross fire. There was a chance that they'd be hit by their own fire. Firing diagonally eliminated danger. It wouldn't be a true cross fire, but it would have to do.

Barrabas turned to look at Hayes, who nodded, and then devoted his attention once again to the trail.

It would be their first hit, the first message to President Trieste that he wasn't dealing only with inexperienced yet zealous rebels. After news of the coming encounter reached Trieste, he would know that he was dealing with professionals. The only thing he wouldn't know was how many.

If Barrabas had his way, he wouldn't find that out until it was way too late.

ACROSS THE TRAIL Alex Nanos said to Billy Two, "You know what I'm thinking about?"

"Knowing you," the Osage replied, "it's not a 'what' that you're thinking about so much as a 'who.'"

"You got that right," Nanos said. "Remember those two girls in Greece?"

Billy Two closed his eyes, then smiled. "I remember."

"That blond-haired one sure went for the fact that you were an Indian."

"And she was a real blonde, too."

"And the other one was a real redhead," Nanos said, remembering the precise moment when she had revealed the evidence of that fact to him.

"What made you think of those two?" Billy asked. "That was two years ago."

"I was just thinking," Alex said, shaking his head sorrowfully, "I ain't seen a real redhead since then." He turned and looked at the Indian and asked, "Have you?"

"No."

"I mean, that stuff that comes out of a bottle, it just ain't the same, you know?"

"I know."

"I mean, it's downright frustrating. You know?"

"I know."

"Here they come," Alex said.

"I know," Billy Two replied, suspecting that just then a little distance away Claude Hayes turned to Barrabas.

"Here they come," Claude Hayes said.

"I know," answered Barrabas.

IT WAS COOLER in the mountains where Lee Hatton was.

She watched as Liam O'Toole drilled former vice president Berbick's supporters with their AK-47s. She thought about Barrabas and the others, down in the jungle making their first contact with President Trieste's troops.

They had received what appeared to be adequate intelligence as to the regular route of Trieste's troops, and the plan was to ambush one such patrol, announcing their arrival to Trieste in the most positive and effective of ways.

Still, she didn't like the idea that there were only four of them down there. She knew that her presence and O'Toole's would not alter the odds dramatically, but she certainly would have felt better if they'd gone along.

She didn't notice that O'Toole had dismissed the men until he came up next to her.

"Worried?" he asked.

She looked at him and shrugged. "Concerned."

"Don't be," he said. "The colonel knows what he's doing."

"Always?"

O'Toole nodded and said, "Oh, yes... always."

"I guess you're right." She looked past him and saw the former vice president of El Salvador, Jules Berbick. He had been watching Nanos put the men through their paces, and the look on his face was one of pure misery.

"What do you suppose he's thinking?" she asked Nanos.

The Irishman looked over at Berbick, and then back at Lee Hatton. "He probably wishes he was somewhere else."

She looked down at the jungle and said, "I know how he feels."

PRESIDENT CAESAR ARMANDE TRIESTE gazed out his office window at California Street. He'd been in office for two months, and each day was even more invigorating than the day before.

He turned and looked at his desk, then let his glance pass appreciatively around his elegant office. His predecessor—whom he had served in the capacity of adviser—had furnished the office, and Trieste had always vowed that when he took over he would keep it just the way it was.

He sat in his chair and poured himself a glass of brandy. It had been two months, and there had been no sign of resistance to his takeover. The only thing needed to make his sense of security complete was for his troops to find Jules Berbick and the mercenaries and eliminate them. Berbick was the only threat to Trieste, but it wasn't because he was a formidable opponent who would muster a great deal of resistance. He was simply the last remnant of Colon's rule to be still around, and once he was gone, the people would accept Trieste as their true president.

Silently he raised his glass in a toast to himself, and to a long and fruitful reign.

JULES BERBICK STARED at the two mercenaries, the woman Hatton and the man O'Toole. He knew that the other four, led by the tall, white-haired man, were down in the jungle, waiting to bushwhack Trieste's men. They were waiting to fight to put him in President Trieste's place in the capital.

They were fighting to make president a man whose last wish in the world was to *be* president of El Salvador.

THE SOBs KNEW from long experience not to fire until Barrabas did. They also knew that Barrabas's steel nerves would keep him from firing until it seemed almost too late.

Luckily, they had nerves to match.

When the patrol came into view, Barrabas raised the stock of the M-16 and sighted on the torso of the first man. He squeezed off a shot and saw the gore spout from the man's chest as he shrugged off this mortal coil—and he wasn't the last.

The others began to fire now, their M-16s set on automatic. On the trail men began shouting, screaming...and falling. Some of them started to fire in return, though they didn't know whom or what to fire at.

Barrabas set his M-16 on automatic and joined in the fray. The men on the trail—the ones who weren't dead—were scrambling for cover now. Eventually a few of them would assert themselves—maybe their commanding officer, if he was still alive—and they'd get themselves organized.

It was time to go, Barrabas decided.

"Colonel!" Claude Hayes shouted.

Barrabas turned and looked at the big black man.

"Another patrol!" Hayes said, pointing.

Down the trail swarmed a group of men, running. That was something Barrabas had not anticipated, to have a second patrol within earshot.

He was not looking forward to facing twenty more men, on top of the group that had just been dispersed.

Now it was really time to go! "Let's move!" he shouted.

They all fed fresh magazines into their rifles and then turned and started a very swift retreat.

It had gone wrong already, which didn't bode well for the future of the mission.

8

On the run, Billy Two took the lead and the others followed. Barrabas brought up the rear and kept an eye behind them. There was no way he could be sure Billy knew where he was going; he just had to trust the Osage—and he did. He and the others followed without a qualm.

Francisco had left behind one of the machetes, and in Billy's hand it became a magic wand, cutting a swath through the heavy underbrush of the jungle for the others to move through. But it was also leaving a path Trieste's men could follow without the least hesitation.

"Hold up!" Barrabas shouted. "Hold it!"

Immediately ahead of him was Nanos, who shouted ahead to Hayes, who stopped Billy Two.

"What's up, Colonel?" Nanos asked. "We can outrun them, you know."

"Maybe, but we're leaving a crystal-clear trail for them to follow. We've got to do something."

"The river," Billy Two suggested.

"What?"

"There's a river up ahead, remember?"

Barrabas remembered the river. They had forded the river with their M-16s and handguns held up over their heads, and the current had been pretty strong.

"I remember."

"Well, if we walk the river for a couple of klicks, we should lose them."

"That current was pretty strong," Barrabas reminded him.

"We can make it, Colonel," Hayes said.

"Even with your hands in the air?" Barrabas asked. It was rough enough walking in waist-deep water that way, off balance in ankle-high mud and trying to keep a weapon dry. Doing it against a heavy current was going to be tricky as hell.

"So we get a little wet?" Nanos said. "We can dry off, clean our guns—we can't do any of that if we're caught...or dead."

"Good point," Barrabas said. "You guys go ahead to the river."

"What are you gonna do?" Nanos asked.

"I'm going to try and give us some time."

Nanos and Hayes exchanged looks. "Let me do it, Colonel," Hayes volunteered.

"No, I'll do it," Nanos said. "I've got a special surprise for those soldiers." With that Nanos removed something from his pack and showed it to them. It was one of the grenades.

"All right, Alex," Barrabas said, putting his hand on the Greek's shoulder, "but don't wait too long. Plant that thing where it will do the most good and come on after us."

"You got it, Colonel."

"All right," Barrabas said. "Billy, let's find that river."

Barrabas, Hayes and Billy Two made for the river while Nanos ran back the way they had come and disappeared in the jungle. When Barrabas and the others got to the river, they stood and watched the flow of water for a minute. If anything, the current looked as if it had gotten stronger.

"Billy, downstream or up?" Barrabas asked.

"Down," Billy Two answered. "It'll be easier to negotiate, and easier to find our way back again."

"Okay," Barrabas said, "let's get the .45s as high up as we can, like inside our shirts. But worry more about your rifle."

Billy Two took out his .45 and put the butt between his teeth. Barrabas and Hayes opted to tuck the handguns inside their shirts. Billy took the lead, stepping into the water, followed by Hayes. Barrabas hesitated, looking behind him for Nanos.

"Colonel!" Hayes shouted above the sound of the rushing river.

Barrabas took one last look behind him, then stepped into the water. Immediately he felt himself being pushed and pulled by the current. With his hands over his head, holding his rifle, he had to fight a tendency to fall forward, so he leaned back against the current.

He would have risked a look behind him if he hadn't thought he would end up getting knocked down.

NANOS WATCHED from a safe distance as the patrol approached the point where he'd rigged the grenades. He got comfortable and fitted the stock of the M-16 to his shoulder.

It didn't take long. Apparently the president's militia were not so well trained, because they had no one walking the point. If that had been the case, then all the grenades would have done was kill one man. Instead, several men approached the rigged wire together, with others close behind. As soon as one of them tripped on the wire, the grenades went off.

Nanos watched as bodies and body parts flew through the air. Before the dust had settled, he fired a couple of bursts to keep the remaining soldiers on their bellies, and then took off on the run for the river. When he reached it, he could barely make out the three figures of the other SOBs. Raising his M-16 over his head, he waded into the water and began to follow them downstream.

BILLY TWO WAS the first one out of the water, and he waited for Claude Hayes and Barrabas to follow.

"Colonel?" Billy Two said, pointing upstream.

Barrabas turned and saw Alex Nanos making his way downstream, his rifle held high over his head.

"Nanos!" Billy Two suddenly called out, and there was a warning in his voice.

Barrabas turned and looked at Billy Two, then back to Nanos. Finally, he saw why Billy was shouting. Behind Nanos on the river was a large tree branch, being carried along at great speed.

"He can't hear me!" Billy Two said.

"And he can't see behind him," Hayes said.

Helplessly they watched, hoping that somehow the branch would miss Nanos—but even as they watched they could see that wasn't going to happen. The branch was unerringly headed straight for Alex Nanos's back, and when it hit they all flinched at the impact.

Nanos disappeared from view, knocked over by the branch and then dragged under by the current.

"I got 'im!" Billy Two shouted.

He shucked his pack and his shoes, stripped off his shirt and dived into the river. While Barrabas and Hayes watched, Billy Two made his way upstream, wading against the current. He had his arms spread wide, obviously hoping to catch Nanos as the current carried him downstream. The only problem with that tactic was that if Nanos had been knocked toward the center of the river, the current would carry him past Billy Two.

Barrabas and Hayes quickly dropped their packs, stripped off shoes and shirts and waded into the water. They spread out behind Billy Two, hoping to cover as much of the river as possible.

Barrabas moved in behind Billy Two and pushed him toward the center of the river while Hayes worked his way to the other side. Billy Two was the most powerful swimmer of the three, and the water in the middle was much deeper. While Barrabas and Hayes were wading, Billy Two was swimming, treading water, hoping to catch Nanos as he went by.

Suddenly Barrabas spotted Nanos, floating between himself and the Osage. Hayes also saw him and started working his way back across the river.

Barrabas moved in Nanos's direction and was there to stop his progress downriver. But the current, combined with Nanos's deadweight, made it difficult to hold on to the inert body. He hooked his hand into Nanos's belt and struggled against the drag while Billy Two moved over toward them. With his other hand he loosened Nanos's pack so that it fell off and went swirling downstream.

Finally, Billy Two reached out and caught one of the Greek's arms, and his strength was such that Barrabas immediately felt the pressure taken off his own arm. In moments, Claude Hayes was also there and together the three of them pulled their comrade from the water.

When they got Nanos ashore, Barrabas immediately began to work on him, trying to get the water out of his lungs and hoping to get him breathing again. Billy Two and Hayes knelt on either side of Nanos, watching anxiously.

Presently Nanos began to choke, and river water started to gush from his mouth. Barrabas exerted a little more pressure until Nanos was taking ragged breaths, and then he backed off, giving the Greek a chance to breathe on his own.

Slowly Nanos rolled over and propped himself up on his elbows. "What the hell—"

"Check him out, Claude."

"Sit still," Hayes said to Nanos.

He checked Nanos out thoroughly, asking him questions. How did he feel? Did his arms or legs hurt? How about his head? His back?

"No bumps on the head, Colonel," Hayes said. "Near as I can figure, the branch hit him in the back, knocking the wind out of him. He went under, swallowed water and became unconscious."

"How does that sound?" Barrabas asked Nanos.

"Okay, I guess," Nanos said. "I don't remember much. I did feel something slam into me from behind, but I thought I was shot."

"Come on, stand up," Barrabas ordered. "See if you can move around."

"I'm all right, Colonel," Nanos insisted. He stood, winced and grabbed his back.

"Can you walk?"

"I'll make it. I lost my rifle, though, and my pack."

"No problem. We'll re-outfit you when we get back to camp."

Barrabas turned to Billy Two. "You know which way to go from here?"

"Well," Billy said, "I'm afraid we have to be on the other side of the river."

"You mean I have to go back into the water?" Nanos asked.

"Well, we're all wet, anyway," Barrabas said. "Come on, let's move out. Alex, stay close to Billy as we cross."

"I want to thank you guys—"

"Save it," Barrabas said, "for somebody who gives a shit."

To take the sting out of his words he clapped the Greek on the shoulder, and Nanos grinned and said, "Yes, sir."

It was lucky for the SOBs that there was enough sunlight left to dry them off before night fell, or they would have spent a miserable cold night. Even the slightest breeze can feel like an arctic wind when you're soaking wet.

They camped, confident that they had left their pursuers far behind them.

"What went wrong, Colonel?" Hayes asked.

"We didn't know enough about President Trieste to accurately predict what he'd do," Barrabas said. "He sent out backup patrols and sucked me right into it."

"Us," Nanos corrected, "he sucked us in, Colonel."

"You never did learn enough to let your CO take the blame, did you, Nanos?"

"I used to," the Greek said, "but you've spoiled me for that."

Barrabas didn't reply. He knew that all of the SOBs felt that way about him, and he knew how he felt about them. It was rare for any of them to vocalize those feelings.

They all had their weapons stripped and were cleaning them, except for Billy Two, the man on watch. When Nanos took his turn, he'd borrow somebody's rifle. He was lucky he still had his .45, or he would have had to draw a Beretta when they got back to camp.

"What's the plan, Colonel?" he asked.

"When we get back to camp, I'm going to talk to Berbick," Barrabas answered. "He'll be able to give us a layout of Trieste's house and office, and of the city."

"Are we going in?"

Barrabas rubbed his thumbnail over his bottom lip and then said, "Yeah, I think so. I don't particularly want to spend the next few weeks playing slap and tickle with the militia in the bush."

"What about the rebels?"

"No," Barrabas said, "they'd be no good to us—except as a possible diversion."

"There's an idea," Hayes said.

"Yeah, and one to consider carefully," Barrabas said. "The right kind of diversion, and we could walk into the city at our leisure."

Hayes checked his watch and said, "Time to spell Billy Two."

He stood up, picked up his reassembled and dried M-16 and walked into the darkness. Moments later Billy Two appeared. Barrabas gave him some dried meat Francisco had supplied them with for the hike.

"Wish I knew what we were eating," Nanos said. "I didn't have the nerve to ask when it was hot, but now that it's cold it tastes . . . funny."

"Probably dog," Billy Two suggested.

"What?" Nanos said, stopping in mid chew.

"Dog meat gets tough when it's dried out," Billy Two said, chewing his own thoughtfully.

Nanos looked at Barrabas and asked, "Is he kidding me or what?"

Barrabas shrugged. He decided not to take part in the byplay.

"What do you know about eating dog, Billy?"

"I've had it before, better than this, though. We tenderize it—"

"Augh!" Nanos said. "I don't want to hear it."

"You're still eating it," Billy Two observed as Nanos took another bite.

"I'm hungry," the Greek explained. "I'll eat it, but I don't want to talk about it."

"Have it your way."

Ever since he'd been taken by the GRU and put through the mill, Billy Two's sense of humor had gone south—most of the time. Nanos couldn't figure out whether or not the big Indian was kidding him, but decided not to think about it or pursue it further.

Dog meat.

Sure.

"IT'S BEEN TOO LONG," Lee Hatton said.

Liam O'Toole didn't reply. They were both eating and drinking coffee.

"Francisco said they'd be a day behind him," Hatton said, "and it's been two."

"Stop worrying."

"He should have left the Miskito with them. How are they supposed to find their way back?"

"Billy Two is like a homing pigeon, Lee," O'Toole told her. "You know that big Indian will find his way back here."

"Yeah," she said, "I just hope the colonel, Nanos and Hayes are with him."

"They'll all be back."

"Do you really believe that, or are you putting up a front?"

O'Toole looked at her. "I've never had much experience at putting up a front, Lee," he said. "It's not my style."

"That's what I thought you'd say."

"So why'd you ask?"

"I just wanted to hear you say it."

O'Toole and Hatton had been training the rebels since Barrabas and the other SOBs had gone into the jungle, and O'Toole had come to a decision.

Whatever they were going to do, they had better count on accomplishing it alone. The best the rebels could do with their AK-74s was make a lot of noise. All the SOBs had to do was figure out a situation in which that would become handy.

They were eating out in front of their tent, and Francisco came over to join them. "Am I intruding?"

"No, Francisco," O'Toole said. "Pull up some ground."

The Salvadoran rebel sat and faced them squarely. "I am sorry I left them—" he began.

O'Toole cut him off in midsentence. He explained to Francisco that Barrabas was in charge of the operation, and when the colonel gave an order it had to be followed. If he hadn't done what the colonel told him to do, then he'd have had something to apologize for.

"I am sorry—" Francisco began, then he stopped himself. "Perhaps I apologize too much."

"Perhaps you do." Hatton smiled at the man.

"Captain...what will you tell the colonel about my men if—when he returns?"

O'Toole put his tin plate down and picked up his coffee cup. "I'm afraid I'll have to tell him the truth,

Francisco," the Irishman said. "These people are just not ready for any kind of serious action. They'd all be going to their deaths."

"A couple of the women aren't bad," Hatton said, but her humor was lost on the little rebel.

"Is something else bothering you, Francisco?" she asked.

"*Sí, señorita,*" he said. "I have not heard from my brother in too long."

"Your brother?" O'Toole repeated.

"*Sí,* Silvio. He was in Orlando, Florida. It was he who contacted you—or contacted whoever you work for."

O'Toole's mind whirred away. So it was Francisco's brother who had been giving Jessup the intelligence they needed, and now Francisco was worried about him. Well, it was entirely possible that Trieste had discovered that Silvio was in Florida and that the president had sent a member of his death squad to take care of him.

"Maybe he's just got nothing to report," O'Toole offered.

"Even so, he would have sent me a message," Francisco said. "He is dead."

"Francisco—" Hatton said.

"No, he is dead," the man said with finality. "I can feel it, here." He touched his fist to his heart. "He is dead, killed by that butcher, Trieste—the way Presidente Berbick's family were slaughtered."

"I'm sorry, Francisco," Hatton said.

"Do not be sorry for me," Francisco told her, "or for my brother. He died for the cause. He is a hero."

O'Toole didn't bother telling Francisco that there were no such things as dead heroes. Dead heroes were

called martyrs. A hero was someone who found a way
to *be* a hero without getting killed.

"Perdón," Francisco said. There was a misty look in
his eyes as he stood up and walked away with dignity.

"Poor guy," O'Toole said.

"I feel sorry for him."

"Yeah, well, we can start feeling sorry for all these
people if we don't do what we came here to do,"
O'Toole said. "If we fail, they'll all get killed sooner or
later."

The talk of death started Hatton thinking about her
other comrades again. Where the hell were they?

THEY HADN'T GOTTEN LOST.

When Billy Two explained that the river had simply
carried them farther away from their destination, Barrabas knew the big Osage was telling the truth. Billy
Two had never made an excuse for anything in his life.

"Here," Billy asked the others, "recognize this
clearing?"

"Yeah," Nanos said. "Yeah, as a matter of fact, I
think I do."

"We are just about four or five klicks from the camp,
Colonel," Billy announced. "Shall we continue in the
dark?"

Barrabas made his decision immediately. Even four
or five *feet* in the jungle could be dangerous. "No
need," he said. "We'll camp, and walk in the morning."

"I could go ahead—" Billy Two volunteered.

Barrabas cut him off. "We'll stay together, Billy."

"Yes, sir."

"Same watch schedule as last night," Barrabas said.

As they settled in, chewing on cold meat again, Barrabas wondered how O'Toole and Hatton were doing with the rebels. Maybe his assessment was wrong. Maybe some of them would be of use.

He didn't really think so, though. He was just hoping, for the rebels' own benefit, that they'd be able to put them to some use. It was, after all, their fight.

They rotated watch as planned, and once dawn came and they got going, it didn't take long for them to cover the remaining distance. It was still early morning when they walked into camp, to the delight of the rebels, who were jubilant to see them. O'Toole and Hatton were happy to see their colleagues alive and well, if looking a bit bedraggled, and Francisco was reassured that his newfound friends were alive.

A general mood of elation seemed to indicate that the rebels considered the reappearance of Barrabas, Hayes, Nanos and Billy Two as a sign that their rebellion would succeed.

Hernando was the only one who wasn't sure how he felt.

"You guys look like something that came out the wrong end of the dog," O'Toole commented.

Nanos gave O'Toole a sour look and said, "Shit."

"That's what I meant."

"Got any hot food?" Nanos asked.

"I'll get it for all of you," Hatton offered.

"And don't bring me any of that damned dog!"

"Dog?" she asked, looking at Barrabas.

"Don't ask," Barrabas said.

The SOBs walked back to their tent, and Barrabas, Hayes, Nanos and Billy Two got some hot coffee into them, followed by a hot meal. Hatton noticed Nanos studying the contents of his plate before he finally dug in and finished it.

Over breakfast Barrabas related the incidents of the past several days to O'Toole and Hatton, who listened intently. When Barrabas finished his story he looked at O'Toole and asked, "What's been happening here?"

"Nothing," O'Toole said sadly, "absolutely nothing. These people might as well have noisemakers in their hands on New Year's Eve."

"That's what I was afraid of," Barrabas said frankly.

"I've tried everything, Colonel—"

"Forget it, Liam. It's not your fault."

"I know that!" O'Toole said. "It's theirs. They're hopeless!"

"But they can make noise?"

O'Toole laughed. "A hell of a lot of it."

"That may be all we need."

"What do you mean?"

"Let me think about it a little more before I discuss it further," Barrabas said. "I'm going to get some sleep. Wake me in two hours."

"Yes, sir," O'Toole said.

When Barrabas went into the tent, O'Toole looked at Claude Hayes for clarification.

The black man from Detroit shrugged. "He said something about a diversion, but he's still working on it."

O'Toole thought about it, then repeated, "A diversion... Yeah." He rubbed his jaw, and a thoughtful look came over his face. "I guess they could manage to do that," he said, "as long as I can keep them from shooting one another!"

Hayes and Nanos eventually followed Barrabas into the tent for some needed rest. Billy Two had another cup of coffee, but as he did not look to either O'Toole or Hatton as though he would be receptive to conversation, they decided to leave him alone with his thoughts—or whatever was going on inside his head.

"A diversion," Hatton said, as if she were mulling the word over.

"It could work," O'Toole said.

For a moment they exchanged thoughtful glances.

"Let's go drill the troops, Hatton," O'Toole said. "We may have finally found something they can do right!"

9

O'Toole woke Barrabas in two hours, as instructed. Barrabas got off the cot and silently followed O'Toole outside.

"What about the others?" O'Toole asked. He meant Nanos and Hayes, who were still snoring away.

"Leave them," Barrabas said. "Where's Billy?"

O'Toole shrugged. "Walking around, I guess."

"He didn't go to sleep?"

"No."

"Find him and tell him to get some sleep," Barrabas said. "Tell him it's an order."

"Yes, sir."

"I'll be talking to our president-elect, Berbick," Barrabas said. "I'm going to get a rundown on the presidential residence, and as much as I can on the city. What have you been doing with the rebels?"

"Seeing how much noise they can make," O'Toole replied. "Hayes told me that you were thinking of using them as a diversion."

"Yeah, I am," Barrabas said. "Can they do that without killing one another, or getting killed?"

"I think so, Colonel," O'Toole said. "If there's one thing I've noticed about them, it's that they always try and do what they're told. They don't always pull it off, but at least they try."

"All right," Barrabas said. "Let me talk to Berbick, and then we'll have a little brainstorming session."

"Right."

Barrabas hefted his M-16 and walked across camp toward Berbick's tent. On the way he encountered Hernando, who asked him to stop, then stood before him, shifting from one foot to the other, as though undecided what to say.

"What is it?"

"I am worried, Colonel."

"What about?"

"About everything," Hernando said. "I have seen your man O'Toole trying to work with our people. It is not going well, is it?"

"No," Barrabas said, answering truthfully, "it is not going well—but I do have some ideas, Hernando."

"It is no good." Hernando shook his head. "We should give up before we are all killed."

"I thought you were one of the driving forces behind this rebellion."

"This is not a rebellion," Hernando said. "It is an exercise in futility. We do not have enough experienced men to storm into the city, and even if we did, we have a man who does not want to be president."

"He told you that?"

"He does not have to," Hernando said. "I can see it in his face."

"Have you talked to Francisco about this?"

"Francisco is an idealist, willing to die for something he knows cannot be realized. I am a realist, unwilling to die for nothing."

"Give me some time, Hernando," Barrabas said. "I want to talk to Berbick, and then my people. After that,

I'll be ready to discuss things with you and Francisco. If we all agree that your cause if futile, we'll go away.''

Hernando didn't look too sure that he liked the idea.

"What do you say?" Barrabas asked.

"*Sí,*" Hernando said, finally, "all right, *señor*. I will wait."

"That's all I ask."

Hernando turned back in the direction of his tent while Barrabas continued on to Berbick's.

TRIESTE WAS BESIDE HIMSELF with anger. This time, Velez thought, Rodriguez cannot hope to avoid the president's anger.

"My plan worked, did it not?" Trieste asked.

"It did, *mi presidente,*" Captain Rodriguez replied.

"And what do we have to show for it?"

"*Nada, mi presidente.*"

"*Nada?*" Trieste said, slamming both fists down on the desk. "I have six dead soldiers, and three maimed soldiers. Did your men at least see how many mercenaries there were?"

"They did not exactly see," Rodriguez said, "but they said that from the amount of shooting there must have been a great many."

"But they did not see a great many?"

"No."

"How many did they see?"

Rodriguez looked back at his president blankly for a moment. "I did not ask—"

"'I did not ask,'" Trieste mimicked Rodriguez. "Go and ask them, Captain . . . now!"

"*Sí, mi presidente,*" Rodriguez said. He turned so quickly that he almost walked into Captain Velez, who had been standing next to him. Since Velez did not move, Rodriguez stepped around the man and headed for the door.

When he was gone, Trieste sat down and said, "The man is an idiot."

"Yes, sir."

"When this is over, I will replace him," Trieste said.

"Yes, sir."

"And what do you have to report to me, Captain Velez?"

"We have found a man who is said to be a friend of Francisco Melendez."

"Who?"

"Francisco Melendez. He is the brother of Silvio Melendez, the man you had Barrio eliminate in Orlando."

President Trieste gave Captain Velez a sharp, probing look. "You know about that?"

Velez smiled, pleased that he had surprised his leader. "He is in my command. I try to know what goes on with the men in my command."

"I see," Trieste said, stroking his mustache thoughtfully. Could it possibly be that Velez was smarter than he had originally thought? Learning from former President Colon's mistakes, Trieste did not surround himself with men who were more intelligent than himself. Colon had done that and one of those men—Trieste himself—had taken his country and his life away from him.

Trieste did not intend for that to happen to him and decided he would have to watch for Captain Velez, and most likely charge Roberto Barrio with keeping his eye on the captain.

He knew that at least Barrio wasn't smarter then he was—just more vicious.

BARRABAS STOPPED at Berbick's tent and called out for permission to enter. In reply, Berbick lifted the flap himself for Barrabas to enter.

"You have come to continue our talk, eh?" Berbick said.

"Yes sir, that's right."

"You have been to the capital?"

"We were there," Barrabas said. He related to Berbick the encounter they had with Trieste's men, up to and including their escape on the river.

"He is smarter than you thought, eh?" Berbick said. "That one is a fox, Colonel. Do not underestimate him again."

"I don't intend to, sir, but I need your help."

"You need information on the palace."

"Yes."

"Well, it is not truly a palace." Berbick went on to explain that the house was very large, with two floors of offices, bedrooms, various living areas, a den and some other rooms that hadn't been furnished yet.

"There was not enough money in the treasury to furnish them all," he explained.

"Must have been tough," Barrabas said, but without much sympathy.

"I know what you are thinking, but it was the former president—President Colon's predecessor—who furnished the house. When President Colon took office, he decided that the money would be better spent on the people than on that house."

Barrabas didn't know whether he believed that or not, but it did make a nice story. "The house, please," Barrabas said.

Berbick built a mostly mental picture of the house for Barrabas, augmented by a rough sketch that he drew as he talked. Barrabas would retain that picture until such time as he deliberately erased it from his mind.

There was a huge entry hall, with a large staircase leading to the second floor. On the first floor there were only different offices occupied by clerks. Berbick said that Barrabas and his people had nothing to fear from them.

It was the people on the second floor that he had to worry about. That was where the president's bodyguards were, the commander of the militia, the president's aide, and it was also the location of the war room.

"That is how the house was laid out by President Colon."

"Do you know anything about a death squad, or hit squad, that Trieste might have formed?"

"I know that while Trieste was President Colon's adviser he was always telling him to start such a squad, one that could go out and act both secretly and openly. He felt it a good means of striking fear into the people and keeping them from ever rebelling."

"Fear is what makes people rebel."

"Ah, but our Colonel Trieste did not share that belief. He felt that fear, true fear, was what would keep people—how did he put it—in line."

"If he has such a squad, would they be quartered on that second floor?"

"Undoubtedly."

"What about the president's sleeping quarters?"

"President Colon's were on the second floor. I don't think Trieste would change that. A first-floor room would be too accessible to would-be assassins."

"Sir, can you tell me where various rooms are, in relation to the stairway?"

"Of course."

The president's office, Berbick explained, was to the right of the stairway, down the hall, second floor on the left. Directly across from the office was the president's bedroom. Right next to there, on both sides, were the sleeping quarters of the bodyguards.

"Bodyguards," Barrabas said. "Would Trieste have bodyguards, sir?"

"You were supposed to call me Jules, Colonel."

"Would he keep them on?"

"No, they were loyal to President Colon. He had all of Colon's bodyguards put to death publicly. Besides, he did not believe in bodyguards."

"Why not?"

"He said they got too close. He always warned Colon that he would be done in eventually by the men closest to him—and he was."

"Of course, Trieste was talking about the bodyguards, and not himself."

"Nevertheless, it was Trieste who had him killed, undoubtedly by one of his newly formed hit squad."

"It stands to reason," Barrabas said, "that he'd quarter his special squad in the rooms formerly used by the bodyguards."

"I believe so, yes."

"But that doesn't make sense," Barrabas said. "All he's doing is changing the name from 'bodyguard' to 'death squad.' They still have access to him."

Berbick shrugged helplessly.

When Barrabas asked Berbick where the radio room was, the man said that it was to the left of the stairway, the very last door on the hallway.

"How many radio operators are needed?"

"Just one."

"All right." Barrabas, closed his eyes, able to envision the entire layout. He continued to ask questions, some general, some calling for opinions on Berbick's part, until he thought he had as accurate a map of the house in his mind as was possible.

"Well, thank you, sir." The mercenary leader stood up. "You've been very helpful."

"It is you who are being very helpful, Colonel Barrabas. My people—that is, I appreciate it."

Barrabas nodded and left the tent. He wondered why Berbick had balked at referring to the rebels as "his people."

"IT WOULD TAKE all six of us," O'Toole said.

Barrabas had been addressing the SOBs in their tent. He had just finished giving them the layout of the entire house and had asked for suggestions.

"Yes," Nanos said, "one for the radio operator, one for the command post, one each for the rooms on either side of the president, and two for the man himself."

"Two?" Barrabas asked.

"One to go in," Hayes explained, "and one to watch the hall for trouble."

Barrabas nodded. "Anyone disagree?"

No one did. There might be some variations to the theme along the way, but they were in agreement with the basic plan.

"All right," Barrabas said, "that's how I see it, as well."

"No worries on the first floor?" Hatton asked.

"Supposedly not. That's where all the clerks are."

"That's where all the clerks were," Billy Two said, "for the former president."

That was their clue for coming up with a variation.

Instead of two men going for the president, one of them would cover the steps rather than stand right outside the bedroom in the hall. If all the others did their jobs, and the one man watched the stairs, there shouldn't be any surprises in the hall outside the president's bedroom.

"If we hit in the daytime," Claude Hayes said, "the president will be in his office, not in his bedroom."

"Correct," Barrabas said.

"So where could the death squad be?" Nanos asked.

"Either in their rooms," O'Toole said, "or out doing what they do best."

"Killing someone," Billy Two said.

"All right," Barrabas proposed, "if we hit late, but not very late, we might catch the president still in his office and his squad in their rooms. If they're out—or if some of them are out—then it's just as well."

"All of this is fine," Nanos said, "but how do we get to the house?"

"Liam is going to take care of that."

O'Toole smiled. "A diversion," the Irishman said. "My people will be making a hell of a lot of noise in different parts of town. They'll keep the regular militia on their toes."

"Without directly engaging them," Barrabas said.

"Correct."

"Who's going to lead them?" Hayes wanted to know. "We'll all be making for the president's palace."

"Francisco can lead one group," O'Toole said, "and Hernando another. I'm sure I can find someone to take charge of the third."

The Irishman looked at Hatton, who had been working with him, and she nodded and said, "I have some ideas."

Barrabas had some ideas, too, about Hernando, but he kept them to himself for the time being.

Variations were bandied about for the next half an hour, but the basic plan seemed sound enough, and finally Barrabas said, "Let's call this off for now. I want to talk to Francisco and Hernando."

"When should we plan this for, Colonel?" O'Toole asked.

"Not for at least a week, I'm afraid," Barrabas answered. "You'll need time to make sure your people know what they have to do."

"Don't worry, Colonel," O'Toole said, warming to the role of drill instructor, "my people will know."

"That's fine," Barrabas said. "Liam, Billy Two will work with you and Hatton on the rebels."

"Yes, sir."

"Nanos? Hayes?"

"Yes, sir?"

"Perimeter checks," Barrabas said. "If we're found out, I want to know about it well beforehand. You'll each take a Miskito with you."

"Yes, sir," Hayes answered for both of them.

"At night you'll switch off with the others. Draw up a schedule."

"Right."

"I'm going over to talk to Francisco and Hernando." He stood up and grabbed his M-16. "We'll meet again after dinner to firm all of this up."

As Barrabas went out the door, the others stood up, picked up their weapons and proceeded to their assignments.

When Barrabas located Francisco and Hernando, he had the distinct impression that he had interrupted hostilities of some kind. The two men were sitting on their cots, glaring at each other.

"Did I walk in at the wrong time?" he asked.

"No, my friend," Francisco said as he got to his feet. "There has just been a misunderstanding between my cousin and myself."

"Your cousin?" Barrabas repeated. "Hernando is your cousin, Francisco?"

"Yes," Francisco said, "and in spite of the fact that our mothers were sisters and we have the same blood running through our veins, we do not always agree."

"I can see that. Can I ask what it is you do not agree on?"

"Please," Francisco said, "it is a personal matter between my cousin and myself, *señor.*"

"I'm sorry, Francisco," Barrabas said, "but I don't think I believe that. Are you disagreeing about the future of your revolution?"

Francisco shot his cousin a murderous glare and then said something in rapid-fire Spanish, to which Hernando replied in kind.

Francisco turned to Barrabas. "Colonel, I see that my cousin has already approached you with his doubts."

"We did speak briefly earlier, yes."

"I apologize for that, Colonel," Francisco said. "My cousin had no right to speak until we had discussed the matter between ourselves."

"Well, excuse me again, Francisco," Barrabas said, "but I think you and your cousin have been disagreeing for some time."

"I am afraid you are right, Colonel." Francisco shook his head. "My cousin is losing his faith."

Apparently Hernando disagreed violently with that and jumped to his feet, turning with an angry-sounding speech to Francisco. The two seemed prepared to go nose to nose, and Barrabas pushed them apart.

"Hold it, hold it!" Barrabas ordered. "If this were just a family argument I'd get out of here and leave you to it, but it's not." Addressing himself to Hernando, Barrabas said, "Obviously Francisco doesn't agree with you. Does anyone else in camp agree?"

"Yes," Hernando replied, looking past Barrabas at his cousin, "there are those who agree."

"There are more who do not!" Francisco returned.

The two exchanged heated glances, and Barrabas spoke before they could erupt into Spanish again. "Here's what I want, then," Barrabas said. "Each of you get your followers together and meet me outside in an hour. That should give you enough time. Agreed?"

"Agreed," Francisco said.

"Hernando?"

The man in question nodded.

"All right," Barrabas said and turned to leave. "Try not to kill each other before then."

"WE HAD A SMALL FORCE to begin with," Claude Hayes said to Barrabas. "If it splits now, what chance have we got?"

"Our chances go from slim to none," Barrabas said. "We've been in similar situations before."

Barrabas was standing in front of the SOBs' tent, watching as Francisco and Hernando began to assemble their supporters into two separate groups. The other

SOBs were also there, drinking coffee and watching curiously.

"Liam, have you had any hint of trouble in camp?"

"If I understood Spanish, then maybe I would have, Colonel," O'Toole said. "They've all been pretty cooperative with me, and all I know is what our interpreter tells me."

Barrabas watched as the camp divided in two. He saw Jules Berbick, also watching from his tent with a puzzled look on his face.

"The next president appears a little worried," Nanos said.

"Wouldn't you be, if you saw your supporters choosing up sides before your very eyes?" Hayes asked.

"They're choosing up sides, Claude," O'Toole said, "not changing sides."

"We'll see," the black man said.

"Looks like they're about ready, Colonel," Hatton said.

Barrabas studied the grouping for a moment. "What do you think, Lee?" he asked. "What kind of a split are we talking about here?"

"Looks like two thirds to one third, to me," Hatton stated. "About two thirds of the people are behind Francisco."

"That's what I figure."

"Oh, one more thing," she said, coming up to stand right next to him.

"What?"

"All of the women are with Francisco."

"I'll figure out what that means later. I'm going to talk to them. Liam?"

"Yes, Colonel?"

"Who's your interpreter?"

"His name's Ricardo," O'Toole said. He moved closer to Barrabas and stared down at the rebels. "There he is, standing with Francisco's group. The little one with the smashed nose."

"I see him. Liam, I'm going to give some of them a chance to bail out. I'm going to convince the ones who decide to leave to give up their weapons."

"We'll take care of it, Colonel," O'Toole said.

As Barrabas went down to talk to the rebels, O'Toole remarked to Hatton, "I guess you did a better job with the women than I did with the men."

"The question is," Hatton said, "can we still do our job with the people we'll have left?"

"Let's see what they do after the colonel speaks to them," O'Toole suggested. "He can be pretty persuasive sometimes."

"Tell me about it," Nanos said.

They all looked at him.

"I mean, he got all of us together, didn't he?"

They all fell quiet as a kind of hush descended on the camp when Barrabas got into the midst of the rebels.

"Francisco," Barrabas called out, "I need that man, Ricardo, as a translator."

"I can translate for you, Colonel," Francisco offered immediately.

"I'd rather not use you or Hernando," Barrabas said. "Just give me Ricardo."

Francisco nodded and sent Ricardo to stand next to Barrabas. Though even shorter than Francisco, the interpreter was muscular from the waist up, while Francisco was simply wiry and strong.

"Do you speak English well, very well?" Barrabas asked Ricardo.

"Yes."

"So there'll be no problem with understanding me and repeating only what I say?"

"No problem, Colonel."

"Good."

Barrabas turned and addressed the rebels. "It seems that some of you don't feel as strongly about your cause as you once did," he said, and then paused while Ricardo repeated what he'd said in Spanish. Barrabas wondered why Spanish translations always seemed to take longer than the original English versions.

When Ricardo was finished, he looked at Barrabas and nodded.

"We were brought in to help you, as you know, and we think that we will be able to help you, but we can't do it without you. We have a plan, but we're going to need as many of you as possible to pull it off. When we're done, we think that Jules Berbick will be your president."

Barrabas again paused to allow Ricardo to translate.

"I am going to ask those of you who want a new president to step over here in front of me."

In front of the SOBs' tent O'Toole said to the others, "See what I mean about his persuasiveness? Anyone who doesn't step over by him doesn't want a new president."

"That's not persuasive," Nanos said. "That's downright sneaky."

After a brief milling around and checking one another out, only six men of the crowd were left standing off to the side with Hernando. The rest had moved up and were standing in front of Barrabas.

"Hernando?" Barrabas called out.

Hernando put his head together with the men who had remained with him, and then they all nodded and walked over to join the rest.

"Well, good," Barrabas said, although what he truly thought was that they'd just wasted a few good hours.

Or maybe they hadn't.

"Francisco," he said, and the man moved to stand next to him.

"Colonel?"

"Will you remember the six men who were still standing with Hernando?'

Francisco looked over at them, then said to Barrabas, "I will remember, Colonel, but why?"

"Do you trust Ricardo?"

He was sure that Ricardo could hear him, but that didn't matter to him. He simply wanted the question answered.

"I trust him," Francisco said.

"Very good," Barrabas said. "I want someone to keep an eye on Hernando and those six men."

"Colonel, excuse me, but if you do not trust these men—including my cousin—why don't you simply send them away?"

"Where would they go, Francisco?"

"I do not— Oh, I see," Francisco said suddenly. "You are afraid they would go to the capital and betray us."

"Perhaps not all of them," Barrabas said, "and maybe if one of them did betray us, he might not even be doing it on purpose. I simply feel better having them here, and having them watched. *¿Comprende?*"

"*Sí,* Colonel, I understand. It will be done."

"Good. I'll be turning the men—and the women— over to Captain O'Toole again. He will split them into three groups. I want you to lead one group and Ricardo another, and I want you to help O'Toole pick out a man to lead the third group."

"What are you planning, Colonel?"

"Listen to O'Toole," Barrabas said. "You, Ricardo and the third man will have a very heavy responsibility, Francisco. I hope you are up to it."

Francisco hesitated for just a moment and then said, "So do I, Colonel."

Barrabas turned to find O'Toole standing there, having anticipated him. "They're all yours, Liam."

"Thanks, Colonel."

Barrabas walked away from the rebels, heading for the SOBs' tent. He was surprised to find his way blocked by Jules Berbick.

"Colonel, I don't think you should have forced those people to stay."

"I didn't force anyone, sir," Barrabas replied. "I gave them all a legitimate choice."

"Either stay or be branded a coward and a traitor?" Berbick asked. "Is that what you call a real choice?"

"It's the only one I had to play with, sir."

"This is not a game, Colonel."

"War is a game, Jules," Barrabas said, using the man's first name for the first time. "In war there are pieces, and those pieces never have a choice as to which space on the board they are moved to. It's the people moving the pieces who have the choice." Barrabas pointed to the rebel force and said, "I gave those people more of a choice than any game piece normally gets."

"Do you really believe that?" Berbick asked.

Barrabas gave the sky a look for a moment, while he thoughtfully scratched his neck.

"No, sir, I don't. A commanding officer of mine said that to me once years ago, and I didn't agree with it then any more than I do now."

"Then why tell me?"

"Well, Jules, I might not have believed him, but he impressed the hell out of me with the analogy."

Jules Berbick stared at Barrabas for a few moments, and then suddenly the big man was laughing out loud. The hearty laughter attracted the attention of the others in camp, and some of the men joined in, even though they did not know what the joke was. None of the laughter had any real humor in it, but it did serve to break whatever tension there was in the air at that moment.

"Colonel," Berbick said, "you are a shrewd man."

"I try, sir," Barrabas said with a wry smile.

10

For the next week O'Toole, Hatton and Nanos drilled the rebels in three separate groups on what they were to do when the time came. Francisco led group 1, Ricardo group 2, and a woman named Nancy Martinez led group 3. It was Hatton who fought for the Martinez woman to be a group leader.

"She has more smarts and more courage than a lot of the men, but she's got something else I think we can count on," she had told Barrabas.

"What's that?" Barrabas had asked.

"Cool," Hatton had responded. "The lady is like ice, Colonel. Believe me, she won't ruffle, and tell me you don't need that in a leader."

Barrabas had a feeling that there was an implied compliment in there somewhere, but he decided not to pursue it at that moment. "What do you think, Liam?" he'd asked O'Toole.

Hatton did not feel insulted that Barrabas was asking O'Toole's opinion. She respected O'Toole, and knew that it was just part of his role of being second in command.

"Hatton's worked with the women more than I have, Colonel," he replied. "I'll give you my opinion if you insist, but she's more qualified to comment than I am."

"You're qualified to comment on the men, Liam," Barrabas said. "Do you have anyone in mind for the job? Any standouts at all?"

"None," O'Toole responded immediately. "If Hatton feels this strongly about the Martinez woman, I'd go along with her."

"All right, then," Barrabas said, "Martinez leads group 3."

Hatton nodded with satisfaction, and that settled the matter. The other SOBs had no problem with it, and although some of the rebels might have wanted to question the choice, for the most part they accepted the decisions of the American mercenaries.

The three group leaders had been picked for the three-pronged diversion. The time was at hand at last.

BARRABAS'S STRATEGY called for splitting the city into three sectors. At the point where all the sectors intersected was the president's palace.

He wanted to draw as many soldiers as far away from the residence as possible, so that if they did somehow discover that they were the victims of a diversion they wouldn't have time to get back in time to interfere with the SOBs.

Each group was instructed to set off an explosion—a harmless explosion that would at the most cause some property damage. It was stressed time and time again to them that no innocent bystanders were to be injured.

Expectation was that when the soldiers responded to investigate the explosion they would not respond in any force. Probably some of them would be dispatched by radio to investigate, and at their arrival the rebels were to open fire with their AK-74s. They were instructed to maintain their cover and under no circumstances whatsoever to engage the soldiers out in the open. For one thing, Barrabas did not want the enemy to realize just how few rebels they were dealing with.

Once the soldiers were sent to investigate and found themselves attacked by rebels, they would undoubtedly radio for help. When the radio operator relayed the message to the commander of the military that there were rebel attacks at three different locations within the city he would have to split his force into three. Hopefully he would react so as to leave the palace almost unprotected except for a few guards and, of course, the president's private little kill squad.

Once the soldiers were dispatched to engage the rebels, the SOBs could move in on the palace.

The group leaders were instructed to withdraw immediately and make no attempt to fight when they had accomplished their objective of drawing the soldiers away from the palace and engaging them in a seeming firefight. That would do two things. It would help to avoid any fatalities among the rebels, and it would lure the soldiers even farther away from the city.

Nanos suggested that the retreating rebels leave some surprise behind, along the lines of fragmentation grenades. O'Toole was then assigned to instruct two people from each group in the handling of the grenades.

Once the SOBs were in the palace, they would deploy as planned and be successful in removing the death squad and ousting President Trieste from office.

The plan was explained first to the groups as a whole, then to each of the three groups separately, and then finally discussed in detail with the three leaders.

Barrabas felt that if orders were followed to the letter the plan would be successful, but unexpectedly, a glaring omission came to light. "Radios," Claude Hayes pointed out. "We need radios."

"Claude is right," Barrabas agreed. "We'll need two radios, one with us and one with Berbick. Once we take the palace, he's going to have to come in and take control. To do that we have to have the means to notify him that it's safe to enter the city."

"You could not have him with you?" Francisco asked.

Barrabas shook his head. "There would be too much of a chance that he'd get hurt. And for the same reason he cannot be with one of the diversionary groups."

"There's no way around it," Nanos said.

Hatton nodded. "We need two radios."

"How do we get them?" Nancy Martinez asked. The woman had taken to her role as group leader, and had made suggestions and asked questions as though she had been born to it. She was in her forties, a solidly built woman who also managed to look handsome.

Barrabas looked at everyone who was assembled inside the SOBs tent. Maps were laid out on a table that had been fashioned from some chairs crowned by a large piece of cardboard.

"We'll have to go and take them," he replied.

"Well," Billy Two said, "won't that be fun!"

Barrabas decided that a group of four would have to go back to the city and take two radios from a patrol. The raiding party was to consist of the same four who had made the trip before. O'Toole and Hatton were the two that the majority of the rebels knew the best, and so they would stay behind.

"This is going to be a three-day job," Barrabas said, to his team when they were in their tent alone. "There's no way around that. We've got to get there, take the radios and get back.''

"Maybe we should all go," Hatton suggested. "Then we'll all be in position when you do get the radios."

Barrabas considered the suggestion, then rejected it. "There'd be too many of you just waiting around in the jungle for us to come with radios."

"Risky, too," O'Toole interjected. "There's too much of a chance that we'd run into a patrol and there wouldn't be time—or space—for all of us to hide."

It was evening, a week after the diversionary training had been instituted. Prior to that all O'Toole and Hatton had done was weapons training.

"There's a drawback to this, Colonel," O'Toole said.

"What's that?"

"These people are ready," the Irishman told him. "If they have to wait around for three more days, they're going to get antsy."

"We can't avoid it."

"I know that," O'Toole acknowledged. "I'm only pointing out that when they do go in, they might react like an overtrained fighter."

Barrabas knew what he meant. An overtrained fighter leaves his best fight in the gym and has nothing left when he gets into the ring. But Barrabas saw no choice in the matter.

"We'll just have to hope that you and Hatton can keep them sharp until we get back, Liam," he said. Punching O'Toole on the shoulder lightly, he added, "Make sure I've got me a contender when I get back."

"A contender." O'Toole nodded and exchanged looks with Hatton.

"It was your analogy," she said, shrugging.

The final decision made, they dispersed to various tasks, and the following morning Barrabas, Hayes, Nanos and Billy Two left with full field packs. They took one of the Miskitos with them. Francisco wanted to go, too, but he finally saw the wisdom in remaining with his group.

"Stay out of the water," O'Toole told them, but they all knew that the gibe was aimed at Alex the Greek, who took it good-naturedly.

"You going to worry this time, too?" O'Toole asked Lee Hatton as Barrabas and the other SOBs made their way down from the peak.

"About as much as you will, Liam," she said.

THEY RESTED ONLY ONCE and managed to cut forty minutes off the trek.

"Okay, we're here," Nanos said. "Now what?"

"Did anyone notice, last time we were here, if all the soldiers were carrying radios?" Barrabas asked.

The three SOBs looked at one another.

"Now's a nice time to think of that," Hayes said.

What they were all considering was whether every member of the Salvadoran army carried a radio, or just patrol leaders.

"If only the patrol leaders carry them," Nanos said, "then the four of us have to take on two patrols. Now, when it was one patrol I wasn't so worried—but two?"

"We'll have to think of something else," Barrabas said.

"Like what, Colonel?" Hayes asked. "We can't offer to buy two radios."

"There is another way," Billy Two began.

"What is it, Billy?" Barrabas asked.

"Patrol leaders aren't the only ones who would carry radios," the big Indian said.

"Who else?" Hayes asked.

"Guards," Billy Two replied. "Sentries."

"But the only place there'd be sentries," Nanos said, "is at the president's palace."

"That's right," said Billy.

"You're suggesting that we steal radios from the president's guards?" the Greek asked. "That means going into the city—deep into the city."

"I know," Billy said. "I will do it."

"No," Barrabas said, "we'll all do it, Billy."

"We will?" Nanos asked.

"I can do it alone, Colonel," Billy Two stated. "You know I can move quietly."

"I know that, Billy, but I won't let you go in without backup."

"Then send Claude or Alex with me."

"Thanks, pal," the Greek said.

"We'll all go in," Barrabas resolved, doing some fast figuring. "Two of us will take the guards, the other two will back them up."

"Colonel, do we know how many guards there are on the palace?" Nanos asked.

"No, Alex," Barrabas said, "but we're going to find out firsthand."

THE PALACE BECAME a blaze of lights as darkness fell, and President Trieste, safely ensconced in its heart, was listening to Captain Velez's report.

"He died."

"He what?" Trieste asked.

They were discussing the interrogation of the man who was reportedly a friend of Francisco Melendez.

"You killed him?"

"No, sir," Velez replied.

"Who worked on him?"

"Barrio, but it wasn't his fault," Velez said. "The man had a weak heart. We had no way of knowing that."

"Did he tell you anything?"

"Nothing."

Trieste forced air through his lips, making a sound of disgust.

"The man's heart—" Velez began.

But Trieste cut him off. "I know, I know," he said. "All right, talk to that man's friends. Maybe one of them knows something."

"Yes, sir."

"But ask around before you try to torture someone else," Trieste warned. "Find out if they have a bad heart."

"Yes, sir."

Trieste stood up and said, "I'm tired. I am going to my room to read. Have my dinner brought up, and then a woman."

"Which one, sir?"

Trieste waved his hand dismissively. "Any one. Just a woman."

"Yes, *presidente*."

"Where are your men?"

"Downstairs, *presidente*. I will have two of them come up early."

"Do that," the president said, "and make one of them Barrio."

"Yes, sir."

"What do you think of him, Velez?"

"Barrio? He is a loner, sir. The others do not like him, and he feels the same about them."

"I am not asking about his popularity, Captain!" Trieste exclaimed. "What kind of a man is he?"

"Cold, deadly, the kind who enjoys his work. He was extremely angry at the man for dying and ruining his fun."

"Send him up to me."

"After dinner, *presidente*, or after the woman leaves?"

"After dinner, and before the woman, but make sure he's in the next room while I'm eating."

"I will, *presidente*."

"That is all."

Trieste waited a few minutes after Velez left, then went across the hall. He was considering having a door cut into one of the walls of his office to create an adjoining room, and then turning it into his bedroom. Then he'd have to leave either room very little and expose himself less.

He'd learned from history that being out in the open created many opportunities for assassination attempts. He intended to never leave the palace—and with the adjoining bedroom, he'd cut down on his movements about the place. Formal state functions were quite rare—and he was well protected there, because trouble was more likely—but aside from those, anything he needed could be brought in, from food to books to women. He was a connoisseur of none of these things. He enjoyed meats and vegetables simply fixed, American thriller novels and heavy-breasted women.

Tonight he had been slated for enjoying all three, he thought as he finished his dinner.

There was a knock on his door, and he called out, "Come!" On the table next to his plate he had a Russian Makarov pistol, and he put his hand on it.

The door opened to admit Roberto Barrio. He stopped a respectful distance away and asked, "You wished to see me, *presidente*?"

"Yes," Trieste said, removing his hand from the gun. He noticed that Barrio wore a Makarov in a holster on his hip. "How did you know that I had finished eating?"

"You rarely take more than thirty-five minutes to eat, *presidente*. I knew what you were eating tonight, and I gave you thirty."

"Remarkable."

Barrio said nothing.

"Why do you think you are here?" Trieste asked.

"I assume to be chastised for killing the man I was . . . questioning."

"Not at all," Trieste said. "Accidents happen. You could not know that the man had a bad heart."

"I appreciate your understanding in the matter, *presidente*."

"Not at all," Trieste said again. "No, you are here simply because I wanted to talk to you."

"About what?"

Trieste shrugged and rose from the table that occupied the center of the room. It would be cleared by the woman later, when he was through with her. That was how Trieste liked to see his women revert from playthings to useful servants.

"About your future, Roberto," he said. "About your future . . ."

THE SOBS WAITED until 2:00 a.m. before they left the jungle and eased into the city of San Salvador. Keeping to the shadows as much as possible, they made their way through the deserted streets, using the map that Barrabas had in his head. The Miskito had refused to enter the city with them, which was just as well. In the jungle he was priceless, but in the city he'd be useless.

The streets of San Salvador were filled with debris, remnants of past regimes and struggles. The new regime rarely cleaned up after the old regime, it just tried to "clean up." The SOBs ran into some people, but they all did the same thing. They looked the other way. Apparently they were used to people walking their streets with guns.

There were cars on the street, but in all of El Salvador—a country of five million—there were less than 130,000 privately owned automobiles, and that number had to be halved for telephones.

Finally they came within sight of the palace and stopped, taking refuge in someone's front yard—or what had been someone's front yard before the house was abandoned. All the homes in the immediate area looked deserted, some of them recently so. Barrabas had no doubt that Trieste had ordered the occupants to leave their homes and that he had no worries about where the people went to live afterward.

"Billy, you and Alex go around back and watch. Time the guards. We'll do the same up front."

"Yes, sir. Come on, Greek."

Billy Two and Nanos left the doorway and worked their way around to the back of the palace. They watched from somebody's backyard.

The outside of the house was poorly lit by low wattage lighting, but the moon was providing enough light to see—or be seen.

"This isn't gonna be easy," Hayes said into Barrabas's ear.

"Let's wait and see."

They waited, counted and timed. When Billy Two and Nanos came back, they compared notes.

There were two guards in the front, and two in the back. They split the length of the house in half, and each guard covered a section and walked it, back and forth. They met at the end of each walk.

"We'll have to get them individually at the far end, at the same time," Barrabas said. "We can't take one and risk having the other raise an alarm."

"The back is easier, Colonel," Billy Two reported.

"All right, Billy," Barrabas said, "lead the way."

The big Osage led them around to the back, through a backyard to where he and Nanos had done their observation.

"See?" he pointed out. "The lighting is even worse back here. All we have to do is wait until they each reach the far side of the house and take them."

"All right," Barrabas agreed. "You and Alex work your way around to the other side. Are they synchronized?"

"Like a Rolex," Billy Two said.

"I hope so," Barrabas said. "If one of them is off a step, the other might be alerted."

"I don't think they'll be able to hear anything, anyway," Nanos said, "short of a shot."

"We'll take them quietly," Barrabas said.

"Alive?" Billy Two asked.

"I guess that'll be up to them."

"Wouldn't it be funny after all this," Nanos said, "if they didn't have radios?" He looked around, but there was no response to his attempt at humor, and they dispersed to take up their respective spots.

Barrabas and Hayes waited until they felt sure that Billy Two and Nanos were in position.

"I'll take him," Barrabas said, sliding his M-16 over his shoulder, "and you back me up."

"Yes, sir."

"Let's move."

Leaving the safety of the yard just as their man was walking away from them, they sprinted to the corner of the house and flattened themselves against the wall. While Barrabas peered around the corner at the guard, Hayes kept a lookout for anything that could possibly come at them.

As the guard approached, Barrabas reached behind him to nudge Hayes, silently letting him know that it was going down.

The guard walked right to the end of the building— as he had been doing the whole time they were watching him—and as he turned on his heels, Barrabas stepped out and clamped one arm beneath his chin and one across the back of his neck, cutting off his air.

Obeying his first instinct, the guard tried to reestablish his air supply by shoving away the arm at his throat instead of reaching for his gun. By the time he thought of the gun, Hayes had stepped out and taken it from his holster. Barrabas increased the pressure, and gradually the man's resistance faded away until he was deadweight. Barrabas lowered him to the ground, and then checked for the radio.

"Got it," he said. It was easy to find because it was old, a large, cumbersome model that hung in a pocket sewn to the man's belt.

"We'd better—" Hayes started to say when suddenly there was a shot.

"Something's wrong," Hayes said.

"Let's move."

WHEN BILLY TWO SLID his arm beneath his man's neck, fate stepped in and took a hand. A large stray dog came out of nowhere and slammed into the back of Billy Two's legs.

"Wha—" Billy exclaimed. Nanos looked over just in time to see the big Osage trip backward over the dog. It was almost comical the way the big man fell, dragging the guard with him. They both hit the ground, and became disentangled. Billy Two rolled away from the dog, which had been pinned beneath him, and the animal bit him, allowing the guard time to pull his gun before Billy could react.

But it was Nanos who fired the shot heard by Barrabas and Hayes—and everyone else in the presidential residence.

"WHAT?" PRESIDENT TRIESTE said with an alarmed shout, sitting instantly in bed.

The woman next to him stirred. It was unusual for him to want his female companions to stay with him after they had finished clearing the table, but he had felt a strange need for that very thing.

He leaned over and turned on the night table lamp. The woman sat up then and pressed her heavy breasts against his arm. She had not heard the shot and had mistaken the situation.

"Don't lean on me!" he snapped.

The door to his room slammed open, and Roberto Barrio entered, a Makarov pistol clutched in his hand.

"*Presidente.*"

"I am all right," Trieste said. "It came from outside."

"I will go and—"

"No!" Trieste shouted. "Stay with me! Let the others go."

Barrio hesitated, torn between obeying the president and his thirst for action. Remembering their conversation earlier that evening, he stepped into the room and closed the door.

BARRABAS AND HAYES CUT through the nearest backyard and made it to a nearby side street, rather than to the main street in front of the building. They could hear the commotion from the house as people poured from within and lights were turned on.

"Colonel," Hayes said as they ran, "the radio—"

"I've got the radio, Claude!"

"No, I mean use the radio," Hayes urged. "If Billy Two and Nanos got theirs, maybe they'll answer and we can find out if they're all right."

"Good idea." Barrabas turned on the radio and quelled his initial impulse to call for Billy and Nanos by name. Somebody else could be listening. He called them without using their names. He continued for a few moments, then gave up and turned it off.

"They must not have turned it on," he said.

"Yeah," Hayes said warily, "that must be it."

CAPTAIN VELEZ HIT the main street with four of his men while the other guards ran around the house in a helpless fashion, like chickens with lopped-off heads.

"The jeep," Velez shouted, and they piled into the nearest jeep. He remained on the street.

"Which way shall we go?" one of his men asked.

"Pick one," Velez said. "If you're right you'll catch them. If you're wrong—" He shrugged. "Check the city limits."

"Yes, sir."

The man started the jeep, pulled out into the street and turned right.

Velez walked briskly to the back of the house, where soldiers were milling about. He looked around for Captain Rodriguez but did not see him.

He took command and started issuing orders. "Check the nearby yards! Stop running around blindly—and don't shoot one another!"

He walked to where one guard was checking out an inert body on the ground.

"Well?" he asked.

"He is dead, sir."

"Where is the other rear guard?"

"Here," someone said weakly, and he looked at the voice's owner, who was hatless, his hair a mess. The man was gingerly rubbing his neck.

"What happened?"

"I don't know," the guard rasped. "I was grabbed from behind and choked. My gun is gone—"

"Your gun?" the captain said. "This was not done by someone who wanted your gun."

"Captain?"

"Yes?"

"This man's radio is gone."

"His radio?" Velez turned to the other rear guard and roughly patted him down, turning him right and left. "Your radio!"

"It's gone, sir."

"You!" he said to the soldier on his knees. "Give me your radio."

The man handed it over and Velez played with the frequency dial. Finally he heard a voice calling out to someone.

"Greek! Osage! Are you there? Greek! Osage! Are you there!"

He listened for a few moments and then it stopped. He turned to the soldiers standing around him and asked, "What is a greek osage?"

BARRABAS AND HAYES finally reached the very point at which they had entered the city and found the Miskito waiting there. There was no sign of Billy Two or Nanos.

The Miskito spoke very little English, but they managed to get out of him that he hadn't seen the other two SOBs.

"I'll try the radio again," Barrabas said. He was about to turn it on when Hayes said, "Colonel, wait!"

Barrabas looked toward the city and saw two figures running toward them. As they came closer, he could make out that they were Billy Two and the Greek.

"Are you guys all right?" he demanded when his men reached him. He could see Billy Two limping.

"We're fine," Nanos said.

"The shot?" Hayes said.

"Billy got bitten by a dog," Nanos reported.

"And you shot it?" Hayes asked.

"No, no, I shot the guard. He was going to shoot Billy after the dog bit him."

"The guard was going to shoot Billy because his dog bit him?" Hayes asked.

"No, no," Nanos said, "it wasn't the guard's dog—"

Barrabas cut them off. "We can hear about this later," he said. "Right now let's put as many miles between us and this city as we can."

"Sounds good to me," Nanos said.

"Can you make it, Billy?" Barrabas asked.

"Yes," the big Osage reassured him. But there was a toneless quality to his voice that indicated to Barrabas that something was troubling the Indian. Unfortunately, the SOB leader thought grimly, now was not the time for the long-drawn-out questioning session to get the man to confess whatever was ailing him. The issue would have to wait, Barrabas decided, but struggled to contain his feeling that they were dragging around a time bomb of undetermined power. "Let's hit it," he said and took the lead.

11

Barrabas had taken the last watch and woke everyone at first light. The Miskito had not been seen all night and had only just returned. The merc leader had no way of knowing if he'd been up all night, or had simply gone somewhere else to sleep.

"Before we go any farther," Barrabas said, "let's check these radios."

He turned his on and began fiddling with the frequency. Presently he came to a frequency where Spanish was being spoken.

"That's theirs," he said, and turned to the next frequency. "This one will be ours. Turn to number three, Alex, and walk about a hundred yards ahead of us."

"Yes, sir."

Nanos picked up his rifle and the radio and trotted on ahead.

"Greek?" Barrabas said into his radio.

"I hear you, boss," Nanos replied. They'd both been careful not to use names.

After that he and Nanos rattled some one-two-threes and a-b-c's at each other until they all finally caught up with Nanos.

"I guess they work," the Greek said.

"They work," Barrabas said, "and we got them first short out of the box. We may have cut this three-day trip to two. Let's move."

They found the trip back uneventful, and once again they did not stop to rest. On both trips they had come to the point where Nanos's fragmentation grenades had gone off days earlier. It would have been much easier if they had found a couple of radios left there in the carnage, but if there had been any radios in that patrol, they had been cleaned up with everything else.

The SOBs made it back to camp before darkness had completely fallen, to the delight of everyone there.

"Colonel," Lee Hatton greeted them, "we didn't expect you back until tomorrow."

"Things went better than we had expected," Nanos explained.

"You got the radios?" O'Toole asked.

Barrabas held his up and Nanos did the same. "We did."

"Any trouble?"

"Just with a dog," Nanos said. He said it to try and get a rise out of Billy, but the big Osage did not even acknowledge having heard the words.

"Let's get something to eat," Barrabas said, "and then we can tell stories."

"I'll see that you all get something," O'Toole said. "Go on to the tent."

At the tent the SOBs shucked their packs and guns and washed up a bit in a basin. The water came from a nearby stream and was cold and clear.

Some of the rebels appeared with food for them, and they all sat down to eat.

When Billy Two sat he showed no discomfort from the dog bite, but Barrabas knew that didn't mean it didn't hurt. He decided Hatton should check the Osage's wound when she'd have a chance to do it in private, without having to embarrass him in front of the others. Barrabas wanted to make sure the bite didn't become infected, and was also concerned about the possibility of rabies. He'd had a very brief aside with Hatton, and she'd let him know that if the dog had been rabid, there wouldn't be much they could do for Billy. But he decided to just wait and hope for the best. No point in worrying about it now.

While they ate, Barrabas left it up to Nanos to relate the story. The Greek had a flair for storytelling, which Barrabas bowed to. When he came to the incident with the dog, he caught a warning glance from Barrabas and simply reported it straight, without any commentary.

During dinner Lee Hatton leaned over and asked, "What's bothering Billy?"

"That's what I want to find out," Barrabas said. "Nearest I can figure, he's embarrassed at having been bitten by a dog."

"Why embarrassed?"

"I think he feels he's out of favor with Hawk Spirit, who should have prevented it."

"Well, Hawk Spirit or not, I should take a look soon at that dog bite," she said.

"Let me get him inside first," Barrabas said, and she nodded.

After dinner Barrabas rose and said, "Billy, can you come inside for a moment?"

"Yes, Colonel."

Barrabas and Billy Two went into the tent while the others remained outside.

"Drop your pants. I want to have another look at that bite."

The big Osage obeyed, letting his pants fall to the floor.

"Do you have objection to Dr. Hatton looking at it?"

"No, sir," he said quietly.

Barrabas went to the tent entrance and asked Hatton to enter.

"Could you take a look at that dog bite," he said to her.

"Of course."

She got her medical equipment and inspected the wound. "It's not deep. Who treated it?"

"I did," Barrabas told her.

"I might have known," she said. "You did a good job."

"Thank you."

"I'll just change the dressing and put some antibiotic ointment on it."

She did so and then allowed Billy Two to pull his pants back up.

"May I go, Colonel?" he asked.

"Not yet, Billy," Barrabas said. "Doctor?"

"Of course," she said. "I'll leave you alone."

When she left Billy Two turned and looked at Barrabas, his face placid, no hint of emotion showing in his eyes.

"What's the matter?" Barrabas asked.

"Sir?"

"It's not your fault you got bitten by a dog, Billy."

"I know that."

"Then why so glum about it?"

"It almost ruined the mission, Colonel," Billy explained. "I would have been responsible for that."

"And you're not allowed to make a mistake?"

"The Spirit—" Billy began, and then stopped.

"Your Hawk Spirit should have kept it from happening? Is that what you're thinking?"

"Sir, I know you do not believe—"

"I believe whatever you believe, Billy," Barrabas said. "Now let's discuss what it is you believe."

Billy Two stared at Barrabas for a few moments, and then suddenly his shoulders visibly sagged. Just as suddenly, his soul was bared on his face and his leader could see the anguish that lay there.

"I'm afraid—" Billy Two began, then stopped and rephrased it. "I am concerned that my spirit may have abandoned me."

"Because of what happened with the dog?"

"Yes."

"Isn't that putting a little more into the incident than it deserves, Billy?"

"The Greek could have gotten killed, Colonel," Billy Two said, "as well as you and Hayes."

"You could have gotten killed."

"I am not as concerned for myself as I am for you and the others."

For a moment Barrabas was tempted to mock him by calling him a self-appointed martyr and to leave the rest up to the shock effect it would produce in Billy. Then he decided not to play it that way. Instead he moved up close to the big Osage and lowered his voice. "Billy," he said, "this is a team, and the team needs you. We depend on you, you know that."

"We have to depend on one another, Colonel."

"Name one member of this team you feel you can't depend on."

It was a challenge that the Indian was immediately up to. "Me," he said.

Barrabas poked Billy Two in the chest with his index finger. "Who's the leader of this traveling dog-and-pony show, Billy?"

"You are, Colonel."

"That's right," Barrabas said, "I am. I picked you all out myself, didn't I?"

"Yes, sir."

"And I did that because I knew I could depend on you—all of you—no matter what."

"That *was* true, Colonel—"

"It is true, Billy," Barrabas said, cutting him off, "and it'll take more than a stray dog biting you on the ass to make me feel different."

Billy didn't respond.

"Big man," Barrabas said, "you go out and make peace with whatever spirit or god you want, because come tomorrow, my life depends on you."

"But Colonel—"

"That's all, Billy."

"Colonel—"

"That's all!"

Billy stared at Barrabas for a few seconds, with nothing readable in his eyes, then he squared his huge shoulders and left the tent.

Moments later Alex Nanos came walking in. "Colonel?"

"Where did he go, Alex?"

"He just walked past us out into the jungle. Should I follow him, Colonel?"

"No," Barrabas said after a moment, "leave him alone. He'll be fine."

Nanos nodded, then turned to leave. Suddenly he stopped and turned back. "Colonel, when do we get this operation underway for real?"

"Day after tomorrow, Alex," Barrabas said. "We go in day after tomorrow. Tell the others."

"Yes, sir."

Barrabas figured that should give Billy Two enough time to work his way out of his depression and restore his confidence.

"A COUPLE OF RADIOS," President Trieste said to captains Rodriguez and Velez. "All this time gone by, and still you can only tell me that two radios were taken."

"And one man killed, *presidente*," Rodriguez said, but it was as if Trieste had not heard him.

"What would they want with them?" he wondered aloud. "To listen to our transmissions?"

"That would not make sense," Velez said. "We can change the frequency on all our radios so that theirs would be worthless."

"They must have known that," Trieste said, "and yet they took a great risk for two radios. Why?"

"And who were they?" Rodriguez asked.

"There are only two choices," Trieste said. "The Contras, or Jules Berbick's people."

"Not the Contras," Velez said.

"Why not?" Rodriguez asked.

"Because they have not yet recovered from the lack of new aid from the United States. They haven't decided what they want to do about it."

"So it must have been Berbick's people," Trieste said, tapping his fingers on the desk top. "Two radios..." he went on, his fingers tapping harder and faster. Finally he slammed his fist down on the desk and shouted, "But why?"

WHEN BARRABAS STEPPED OUT of the tent darkness had fallen. Nanos was sitting nearby, but the other SOBs were nowhere in sight.

"Alex."

"Yes, sir."

"Where are those radios? I want to try them."

"I'll do it, Colonel."

Nanos retrieved the radios and tried them both on every frequency while Barrabas stood in the entrance of the tent.

"Nothing, Colonel," the Greek reported. "Either they're not transmitting until they can change their frequencies, or these gadgets have a limited range."

"Yeah," Barrabas said. "Well, as long as we can hear each other, that's the whole point."

"Yes sir."

"I'm going to turn in, Alex," Barrabas said. "Tell O'Toole I want to run them through tomorrow, over and over until we're sure they've got it right."

"I'll tell him, Colonel," Nanos said. "It'll be nice to get it over with and get out of here."

"Yes," Barrabas said, "it'll be nice."

"Oh, Colonel?"

"Yeah?"

"Billy's not back yet," Nanos said. "Uh, would you mind if I went looking for him?"

"In the dark?"

"I won't go far."

"He'll be back, Alex, but if it makes you feel better, go ahead."

"Thanks, Colonel."

Barrabas went inside and stripped for sleep. He left the Beretta 93-R and the M-26 within easy reach of the cot, and drifted off.

THEY STARTED DRILLING the three groups of rebels in the morning and continued through the afternoon until they were complaining.

"Tell them to break for dinner," Barrabas said.

"And come back?" O'Toole asked.

"And come back."

"They've been working hard," O'Toole said.

"I know, Liam. So have we."

The SOBs had dinner and when they were ready the three groups were waiting for them.

"Ricardo?" Barrabas called the powerful little group leader over.

"*Sí*, Colonel?"

"Tell them to be ready to leave in the morning."

"That is all?" Ricardo asked. "We are ready to work—"

"No more practice, Ricardo," Barrabas said. "Tomorrow we go to work for real. Tell them."

"I will," Ricardo said.

When the groups had dispersed, Barrabas turned and said to O'Toole, "We'll need one man from each group to stay with Berbick."

"I'll get 'em."

"I'm going to take one of those radios over to Berbick," Barrabas said, "and make sure he knows how to use it."

O'Toole nodded and handed Barrabas one of the radios.

"Liam, figure out what time we have to leave in order to get to the capital by nightfall, and not much earlier. We don't want to have sixty people sitting around waiting for the sun to go down. We'd make too big a target."

"I'll work it out, Colonel," the Irishman said. "I'll have it ready for you to look at when you get back."

Barrabas nodded, then made his way through camp to Berbick's tent. He had to have one more talk with the man to make damned sure the SOBs were not risking their lives for nothing.

Barrabas paused outside the tent, then called out a greeting just before he entered.

Berbick looked up. "Tomorrow is the big day?" the former vice president asked.

"Yes, sir," Barrabas said. "I brought you this."

Berbick stood up and took the radio.

"Do you know how to use it?"

Berbick smiled and said, "Yes."

"When we've taken Trieste, I'll call for you on the radio," Barrabas said. "You'll have to come as soon as I call. Once we get in there, you're going to have to take over immediately."

"I understand," Berbick said. He put the radio down on the cot and sat next to it.

"Let's get straight on this now, Jules," Barrabas said then.

"On what, Colonel?"

"On tomorrow," Barrabas said. He let some time go by, and then he asked, "Are you going to be there?"

Berbick looked at Barrabas and said, "I don't think I understand."

"The question is simple enough," Barrabas said. "Are you going to be there tomorrow?"

"At the capital? Of course I will be there."

"I mean when it counts, Jules." Barrabas leaned over and tapped the radio. "I mean when I call you on the radio and I say, 'Jules, come and get your country,' are

you going to be there? Tell me the truth now, because
there's no point in risking my people."

"I don't—"

"You're not sure," Barrabas said. "To me that's the
same as saying no." Barrabas leaned directly over Berbick. "Be certain by tomorrow morning, Jules. Make
up your mind one hundred percent before we leave, because once things start rolling, there's no turning back."

"What do you mean?"

"I mean that when I call for you on the radio, you'd
better come."

"And if I do not?"

Barrabas straightened up. "I'll let you imagine what
the answer to that one would be," he said. He walked
to the tent flap, then turned and said, "Good night, Mr.
President."

THE OSAGE SAT on his haunches in the jungle with his
eyes closed. He was listening for the spirits. He had been
there all day, walking and searching, sitting and listening, waiting for the great Hawk Spirit to come to him
and explain.

He waited a long time, and Hawk Spirit never showed
up.

So he explained it to himself.

ON THE WAY BACK to the SOBs' tent Barrabas saw Billy
Two emerging from the jungle. When Billy saw him,
they both stopped, then the Osage came toward him.

"Billy," Barrabas said.

"I just wanted to tell you I'll be ready tomorrow,
Colonel."

Barrabas nodded, and Billy made for the tent ahead
of him.

But Barrabas didn't budge and called out quietly. "Billy?"

The big man turned to face the merc leader, and Barrabas smiled. "I think you're ready right now."

PRESIDENT ARMANDE TRIESTE was restless. Even though he had used the big-breasted woman in bed with him twice, he still could not sleep. It was as if something was keeping him from becoming tired.

The question of the radios still bothered him. Already their frequencies had been changed, so the rebels could not pick up any information from that source. But that was to be expected, for sure. Why then did they take them? There had to be a reason to justify the risk involved in taking them, but he couldn't come up with an answer.

Something was in the wind. He could smell it. He had instructed Captain Velez to keep his squad close to the house at all times. Trieste knew that Roberto Barrio was in the next room, and that the others were in the vicinity.

He was safe, he thought, turning to the woman and placing his hand on her hip, safe in his own house, in his own bed.

But he still could not sleep.

IN THE NEXT ROOM Roberto Barrio sat in a chair. He could have lain down on the bed if he wanted to, could even have dozed off, but he chose to sit in a straight-backed wooden chair, listening, thinking.

Waiting.

Something was going to happen. He could feel it, and he wanted to be awake and ready to make the right move.

The right move . . . for himself.

BARRABAS ENTERED THE TENT and found all the SOBs seated on their cots.

"Liam?"

"With the size of our party, Colonel, we'll have to leave before dawn to get there by dark."

Barrabas nodded.

"Do you want to check my figures?" O'Toole asked.

"There's no need, Liam," Barrabas said. "I've already figured it, and I agree. I'll let you all turn in as soon as we go over our plans one more time."

And so Barrabas started from scratch and walked his SOBs through the action, up to and including the point where he took his radio and called for Berbick.

"Is he going to come, Colonel?" O'Toole asked at that point. "I mean, he's been pretty wishy-washy on the subject up until now."

"He'll come, " Barrabas said. "He'll come and take over as president."

"Once he does, our job is done, right?" Nanos asked.

"Yes."

"What do we do then, Colonel?" Hayes asked.

"Then?" Barrabas said. "We get the hell out of this country before somebody else comes and takes it away from him."

IT WAS STILL DARK when Barrabas dispatched the SOBs to wake the camp. Soon the area swarmed with activity as the rebels got ready, gathering into the individual groups.

"Liam," Barrabas said at one point, "I want Berbick to travel with group 1."

O'Toole nodded and went to arrange it.

When they were ready to move, Barrabas came out and, through Ricardo, explained just how they would make the trip.

Barrabas and his SOBs would take the lead, along with a Miskito Indian. Group 1 would then move out second, led by Francisco. They would be responsible for the safety of Jules Berbick during the trip.

Group 2 would leave second, and then group 3 would bring up the rear. The merc leader explained that he wanted at least twenty yards between groups at all times. That way, if one group got attacked, the others would be able to get away. He instructed each group to look after itself, and no one else. If one group was lost on the way, the others would still be able to pull off the mission.

Through Ricardo he asked if there were any questions, and then if anyone had changed their minds about going. No one stepped forward, but after a few moments, Francisco approached Barrabas.

"What is it, Francisco?"

"It is my cousin, Colonel."

"Hernando?" Barrabas said. "What about him?"

"He is not here."

"He's left camp, you mean?"

"Where could he have gone?" Francisco asked. "Can we wait for him?"

"We can't wait, Francisco. He must have changed his mind about going."

"Of course, you are right," Francisco said. "We cannot wait. I will get back to my group."

As Francisco went to join his men, Barrabas moved over to where the SOBs were standing. "Billy, can you find your way to the capital?"

"Yes, sir."

"All right, take Nanos and get moving. Without the rest of us you'll be able to move a lot faster."

"What are we looking for, Colonel?" Nanos asked.

"I'm not sure," Barrabas said, "but I think maybe Hernando."

"You think he might be on his way to betray us?" Billy Two asked.

"It's a possibility," Barrabas said, "and it's one we can't afford to overlook."

HERNANDO PAZ RAN through the jungle as quickly as he could. He had been a fool to listen to his cousin, Francisco. There was no way six American mercenaries and fifty farmers could defeat President Trieste's army and put Jules Berbick in the presidential palace. They would all be taken captive or killed, and the ones who were caught would be tortured for the names of every man in their force.

Hernando had only one chance to save his own life. He had to get to the capital ahead of the opposing force and explain to President Trieste that he had nothing to do with opposing him. By giving up the others—even his cousin Francisco—he would save his own life.

That was how badly Hernando Paz wanted to live.

12

Billy Two and Alex Nanos pressed on through the jungle in the dark. The Greek moved surely behind the big Indian, certain that the Osage knew exactly where he was going. Once dawn came, they'd be able to pick up the pace. They had left their packs behind since they would move better without them. Barrabas said they'd have all the supplies that were needed with the groups.

They had established a steady pace when suddenly something snagged Nanos's foot and he went down with a crash.

Billy Two stopped immediately and turned back to help the Greek up. "Are you all right?"

"I'm fine." Nanos brushed himself off. "I just tripped over something."

"You have to be careful," Billy Two warned. "You have to step where I step."

"Right, Billy, right," Nanos said. "Come on, keep going. If I fall down again, I'll pick myself up. I been doing it since I was two years old. Okay?"

"Sure," Billy Two said, "sure. Just don't step into any quicksand or anything. You haven't had any experience with that stuff."

"Okay, if I step in quicksand you can help me, otherwise keep going. Deal?"

"Deal," Billy Two said, and they set out again.

THE PROGRESS of the main force was slow. The SOBs and the Miskito were able to maintain a steady pace, but the three groups straggled laboriously and uncertainly through the jungle.

"What if Hernando gets there ahead of us?" O'Toole asked as he walked beside Barrabas.

"We'll have to hope Billy and Alex catch up before he can get to Trieste."

"I don't get it," O'Toole said. "What does he want to gain by giving up all his friends?"

"His life," Barrabas answered. "He's looking to save his own life, because he doesn't think this particular little rebellion is going to succeed."

"And do we think so?" O'Toole asked.

Barrabas looked at him. "Oh, yes, we sure do. We're going to make it succeed."

"I like it when you're this confident, Colonel," O'Toole said. "It makes me feel a whole lot better."

"Just shut up and walk."

JULES BERBICK PLODDED ON through the dense vegetation with determination. Colonel Barrabas's visit to his tent the night before had finally brought home his responsibility to the people who believed in him and were willing to fight for him and risk their lives. And he'd also been brought face-to-face with his responsibility to live up to himself.

No matter how much he wished he was somewhere else, he would do his very best to move along at a brisk pace with the rest of them, and be ready when Barrabas's call came over the radio.

That morning Berbick had gone to Barrabas just before they were leaving, and had told the American of his hard resolution.

"I'm glad to hear all of this, Jules," Barrabas said. "I'm sorry if I seemed unduly hard on you last night—"

"Not at all, Colonel," Berbick assured him. "You brought me to my senses. You did us all a service. I do ask you one thing, though."

"What's that?"

"I'd like to have a gun."

"Do you know how to use a gun?"

"A handgun, yes."

"Very well. I'll get you a Beretta."

Berbick had nodded his thanks, and after a quick stare into each other's eyes, the two men had exchanged a firm handshake.

Now Berbick touched the Beretta that was tucked into his belt. The first chance he got he was going to point the weapon at Armande Trieste and pull the trigger until the gun was empty.

That was the responsibility he had to himself.

Revenge.

PRESIDENT TRIESTE WAS in a foul mood. He had spent the morning biting off the heads of his staff.

First he'd had a go at Captain Rodriguez. "I want soldiers all over these streets, Rodriguez, and anyone who even looks funny I want thrown into jail!"

"But the law—"

"*I* am the law, Rodriguez! If you don't know that, then perhaps *you* belong in jail!"

"*¡Sí, presidente!*" Rodriguez said. "I will do as you say!"

Next it was Captain Velez's turn.

"I don't want any of my squad out of this house, do you understand?"

"*Sí, presidente,* I understand."

"They're to stay here unless I say otherwise."

"*Sí,* just as you say, *presidente.*"

"And I want Barrio in here... now!"

"Are you expecting trouble—"

"Those two radios had to be taken for a reason!" Trieste shouted. "I don't know what the reason is, but yes, I am expecting trouble. Now send me Barrio!"

When Barrio came in Trieste said, "You are not to leave my side, do you understand?"

"I understand."

"Where I go, you go, Barrio. Don't let me out of your sight."

"I will do as you ask, *mi presidente,*" Barrio said, and it never occurred to Trieste that there was a mocking tone to the man's obedient response.

Barrio privately wondered what would happen if the trouble the president was expecting today did not come.

How long would it take for the man to go mad?

HERNANDO'S LUNGS BURNED as if someone had set them afire. He had to stop running, just to rest for a while. Staggering to a stop, he found a rock to sit on.

He sat on the hard surface, the blood roaring in his ears while he heaved in great gulps of air, oblivious to the shifting of shadows around him and the faint rustling of leaves.

DAYLIGHT CAME and Billy Two and Nanos kept up a relentless pace, trying to catch up with Hernando. Nanos, too, after he'd stumbled headlong, became more surefooted.

Billy Two seemed mindless in his pursuit, and although Nanos's breath was coming in rasps, the big

Osage seemed unaffected by the long run. Still, so far Nanos had managed to keep up. He must have been in better shape than he'd known, the Greek thought a trifle smugly.

Nanos was wondering how far ahead of them Hernando was, and what progress Barrabas and the others had made, when Billy Two stopped so suddenly that he ran into his back.

"What the—"

"I smell something.'

"What?" Nanos said dubiously.

"Blood."

"Listen—" Nanos started to say. He'd been about to question the big Indian's sense of smell when suddenly the smell wafted to his nose.

It *was* blood.

Silently he moved to the right of the path. Billy Two went to the left.

It was Nanos who found the rock.

"Psst," he called. When Billy Two appeared, Nanos pointed to the rock. It was a light-colored rock with a slick surface—a surface that was now splattered with blood.

Billy Two moved closer to the stone, then looked beyond it. "It looks like something was killed here and then dragged into the jungle," he said. "Come on."

"Sure," Nanos answered, although he was dubious about tracking something that might have been big enough to drag a man into the jungle.

They only had to follow that trail for a few yards.

Nanos looked on speechlessly for a minute.

"Well," he said finally after a last glance at the mauled and chewed body of Hernando, "I guess he won't be betraying anyone."

WHEN BARRABAS SPOTTED Billy Two and Alex Nanos, the big Osage was standing and the Greek was squatting. The only thing calling for concern, though, was that they weren't moving.

"What's happened?" he asked them.

"We'll show you," Nanos said, standing up. He and Billy Two took the other SOBs off the trail to where they had found the body of Hernando.

"Hell," Hayes said, and Lee Hatton turned away.

"What was it?" O'Toole asked.

Nanos shrugged and Billy Two said, "Some kind of a cat. Jaguar, probably. Looks like some smaller animals might have come by after the big one finished feeding."

"Poor jerk," O'Toole said.

"Should we bury him, sir?" Billy Two asked.

"Hardly enough left to bury," Barrabas said, "and we've got a schedule to keep."

They moved away from the body back to the path.

"You fellas need a rest?" Barrabas asked.

"No, sir," Nanos said, "we rested waiting for you."

"All right, then let's keep moving."

"What about Francisco?" Lee Hatton asked.

Barrabas looked at her. "We'll tell him," he said. "Afterward."

They continued their trek, crossing now familiar rivers and swamps. As darkness began to approach, Barrabas could tell from landmarks that they were nearing the city. When they came to a clearing he called the SOBs to a halt.

"We'll wait here for the others," he said. "Just for something to do, check your weapons. Billy, keep watch."

They passed the time, each of them wrapped up in thoughts of what lay ahead as complete darkness descended. They had been waiting for nearly an hour for group 1 when O'Toole came to a conclusion.

"We miscalculated, didn't we?" O'Toole said to Barrabas.

"Yes," Barrabas said. "Both of us."

"What do you mean?" Hatton asked.

"We calculated when we'd have to leave for the six of us to get here by dark," Barrabas said. "We did not take into account that we'd be traveling in four separate groups."

"So by the time group 3 arrives," she said, "who knows what time it will be."

"Right," Barrabas said, "and we need the cover of darkness to make this work."

"We have to wait for them, then," Hayes said.

"And hope they don't get lost," O'Toole added.

In five minutes group 1 arrived.

While O'Toole checked to make sure Berbick was in good shape and that all members of the group had made it, Barrabas calculated the other groups' probable arrival times.

"The others should be here at half-hour intervals," he said. "That still gives us enough time to pull this off. Meanwhile, let's start moving into position. Jules?"

"Yes," Berbick said, stepping forward.

"When you're in position contact me by radio—"

"I will."

"Wait, let me finish. We'll be listening. Just say the words 'home free.' Trieste must be having all frequencies monitored. Do you understand?"

"Yes."

"After that you will monitor our frequency, and when I say 'It's a go' you will proceed with your diversion."

"Yes."

"And remember," Barrabas said, "you hang back when the diversion starts. I don't want you involved in the shooting. Is that understood?"

"Perfectly."

"The other groups will proceed only when you've set off the explosions. Francisco, do you have your grenades?"

"Yes."

"Are you clear on how to use them?"

"We are clear."

"Then get going. Good luck."

"And to you."

Group 1 moved out, and the SOBs settled back to await the arrival of Group 2, which occurred twenty-nine minutes later under the leadership of Nancy Martinez. Barrabas had already heard the words "home free" over the radio, so he knew that Berbick's people were in position.

"Have the others arrived?" she asked.

"Group 1 has arrived and by now should be in position," Barrabas replied. "Now it's time for you to do the same."

"We will leave immediately."

"When you hear the first explosion, Martinez," Barrabas said, "that will be your signal to move. Do you understand?"

"I understand, Colonel."

"Then good luck."

She nodded and group 2 moved out.

The next interval elapsed, and the third party had not yet arrived. Barrabas calculated that group 2 must have accomplished its initial task.

When group 3 was forty minutes late, O'Toole said what they were all thinking. "They either got lost, or—"

"Or they encountered a patrol," Barrabas concluded. "We'll have to go ahead without them."

"Can we do it with two diversions?" O'Toole asked.

"We have to," Barrabas said, "or give it up." He looked around at the other SOBs questioningly.

It was left up to Alex Nanos to state the group consensus. "Well, I guess two diversions are better than three."

The SOBs advanced through the jungle until they reached a point where they could see the city.

"Are we all ready?" Barrabas asked.

There were nods and whispers of assent from the others.

Barrabas raised the radio to his lips.

"IT'S A GO," the radio operator heard a voice say, and he immediately called out, "Captain!"

Rodriguez rushed into the operators' room.

"A voice just said 'It's a go,'" the man repeated excitedly.

"And what did the other one say?"

"Earlier a voice said "'Home free.'""

"Was it the same voice?"

The man hesitated, then said, "I couldn't tell, Captain."

"Very well. Keep monitoring. I will inform the president."

Rodriguez left the room and hurried down the hall to the president's bedroom. He knocked and entered, knowing that Trieste would still be awake.

"What is it?" Trieste asked from his bed. He glanced at Roberto Barrio, who was sitting quietly in a corner.

"Another transmission, *presidente*."

"What did it say?"

"This one said 'It's a go,'" Rodriguez answered.

"What does that mean?" Trieste asked.

Rodriguez stared at his president and then said, "I— I don't know."

"It is an Americanism," Barrio started to say from his corner, and when he was sure he had the attention of both men, he continued. "It means that whatever is being planned is proceeding according to plan."

Just as they exchanged glances with one another, an explosion shattered the silence of the night.

They froze, momentarily shocked by the unexpected sound, but a second explosion broke the spell.

Rodriguez turned and dashed into the hall, heading for the radio room. Trieste leaped out of bed and, as Barrio headed for the door, the president shouted, "No, no, no! Don't leave."

"I have to—" Barrio started to say, but Trieste would not let him get the words out. He ran over to the younger man and grabbed him by the shoulders.

"You will stay with me, Barrio, and if I come out of this night alive, you will be vice president!"

Barrio stared at Trieste for a long moment, and when he saw that the man was serious, he slammed shut the door of the president's bedroom and took out his Makarov.

SOLDIERS WERE DISPATCHED to find the sites of the two explosions and investigate. Their instructions were to radio back to the presidential palace when they had located and identified the problem.

Fire and smoke led them to the sites, and the crowds that had gathered at those locations pinpointed the trouble spots.

The crowds were going to be a problem, Francisco thought as he watched nervously the street filled with people. His instructions from Barrabas were specific. No innocent bystanders were to be hurt by their action.

Suddenly two jeeps appeared down the street, crowded with soldiers.

"Here they come," a man said to Francisco. He was Julio, Francisco's second in command.

"I see them," the group leader said.

"Do we shoot?"

"We shoot," Francisco said, "but we must aim over their heads."

"Over their heads? What good does that do?" Julio demanded. "We came here to—"

"To do what the colonel told us. We will shoot over their heads until the street clears of bystanders. Then you can pick your target."

As the jeeps pulled to a stop, Francisco raised his AK-74. When the soldiers leaped from their jeeps, Francisco fired, which was their signal for the others to commence firing.

The soldiers scrambled behind their jeeps, and the bystanders scrambled for cover. From behind the safety of their jeeps the soldiers radioed for help.

NANCY MARTINEZ and her group went through the same process, except they did not have to worry about crowds in the street. The location for the second explosion was not as populated as the first. When the soldiers arrived in the jeep, she and her people opened fire, hitting two of them and sending them spinning to the ground. The other two ducked behind their jeep to radio for help.

"CAPTAIN! CAPTAIN!" the radio operator shouted.

Rodriguez rushed into the radio room.

"Our men are being fired upon."

"Rebels," Rodriguez said. "Where?"

"At both locations."

"Send two companies to each location. I want the remaining men to stay here."

"Yes, sir."

Rodriguez wanted to leave and go with one of the companies, but he had to stay to coordinate.

"Where is Captain Velez?" he asked the radio operator.

"I do not know, sir."

Rodriguez turned to a soldier standing nearby and said, "Find Captain Velez."

The soldier fired off a quick salute and wheeled around to fulfill the command.

THE FIRST EXPLOSION had sent the SOBs traveling through the darkened streets of the city, three on each side rather than all on one side. They were aware that there was a lot of activity in two other sections. Enough, they hoped, to lure most of the soldiers from the palace. Barrabas was hoping that the rebels would obey his orders rather than get carried away and engage the soldiers in open battle.

He retraced the route they'd taken the night they had stolen the radios. When they finally reached a point where they could see the president's residence, he called the SOBs to a halt.

The place was lit up inside, but the outside lights were the same. They had not been increased with the addition of floodlights. There was enough light for the soldiers on guard around the house to be visible.

"How many do you count?" Barrabas asked O'Toole.

"Close to thirty."

"Thirty," Barrabas said. "And probably more inside, including the president's special squad. Those are the soldiers who would have been drawn away by that third explosion."

"What do we do now?" O'Toole asked.

Barrabas had just opened his mouth to reply when suddenly a third explosion rent the air.

"Ricardo!" Barrabas said.

"All right!" O'Toole exclaimed. "He found his way!"

"Now let's see what effect this has on the soldiers," Barrabas said.

RODRIGUEZ DEBATED what to do for a while before he made his decision to commit men to investigate the third explosion.

"How many?" the radio operator asked.

"The rest of them," Rodriguez said. "We'll protect the president ourselves."

By that he meant the soldiers assigned to the house—the radio operator, and some guards and clerical people.

"What about Captain Velez and his men?"

"That's right, they'll be here, too," Rodriguez said, "if we can find Captain Velez."

The radioman transmitted the instructions, and with a show of haste soldiers started to load into jeeps.

The last jeep was just pulling away when Captain Velez and his men arrived.

For a minute he stared after the departing vehicle in disbelief. "The fool!" he said, and ran up the steps to the house with his men behind him. Only Barrio, who seemed to have become the president's personal body-guard, was missing from the squad.

He charged up the stairs to the radio room where he found Captain Rodriguez.

"Where have you been?" Rodriguez demanded.

"We were rounding up some suspects. We went to the scene of the first explosion, but you have plenty of soldiers there—too many, in fact."

"What are you talking about?"

"Don't you realize what's happened?" Velez said. "You fool, you've fallen for a diversion!"

"That's nonsense," Rodriguez said. "The rebels are attacking our city and you call it a diversion?"

"How many men do you have here?"

"Counting you and your men, perhaps twelve."

"Not enough," Velez said. He looked at the radio-man and said, "Call two companies back here."

The radioman looked at Rodriguez, who shook his head.

"Well, one then!" Velez said, and still Rodriguez shook his head. "You're making a big mistake—"

"You and your men are supposed to be such a 'special' squad," Rodriguez said. "Well, now is your chance to prove it."

Velez and Rodriguez locked eyes, and it was Velez who finally looked away in disgust.

"Fall behind," he barked to his men and headed for the president's suite.

TRIESTE HAD his private squad at attention before him. He had moved over to his office to sit behind his desk in this time of crisis.

"You are all to stay in the house," he told them. "Send the others outside."

"Rodriguez—" Velez began.

"I'll take care of Rodriguez."

"You'll want the radio operator to stay—"

"Everyone!" Trieste shouted. "Everyone out but you and your men!"

"Yes, *presidente*," Velez said, but he didn't agree with the decision.

As they started for the door, Trieste said, "Barrio stays with me."

Velez looked at Trieste, then Barrio, then back to the president and nodded.

"Get everyone else out of the house and fighting in the street!" Trieste shouted. "And then I want you all back here to protect me!"

Velez and his men exited the office and walked down the hall toward the radio room. Rodriguez looked out the door and watched their approach. The look on Velez's face told him all he needed to know.

"Rodriguez," Velez said at the door, "the president wants you and all remaining men outside the house, and immediately!"

"All of us?"

"That's right."

Rodriguez shook his head. "It is crazy."

"That is what the president wants."

Rodriguez stared at Velez and knew that the man was telling the truth. "Velez, the radio operator—"

"Him, too."

"But we need to be in constant communication with—"

"Those are the president's orders, Captain Rodriguez."

"But ... you don't agree with it either, do you?" the other man asked.

Velez hesitated a moment. It would be the first time he could remember that he and Rodriguez agreed on something. "No, I do not, but he is the president."

"Granted," Rodriguez said, "but let's leave one man here on the stairs. He'll be able to see the front doors, and also hear the radio. What do you say?"

It took Velez only a moment to agree.

"HOLD IT, HOLD IT!" Barrabas said and waved his arm in a restraining manner.

The front door of the house had opened and seven armed men had emerged. With the two guards already outside, that made nine men they had to get by.

"Don't tell me Trieste's staying inside alone," O'Toole said.

"No, I don't think so," Barrabas replied. "I'd be willing to bet he's still got his squad inside."

"So if we get past those nine," Hayes said, "we still have to deal with them."

"We'll have to take them without any fuss," Nanos said, "or the radio operator will recall the other soldiers. Then we won't have a chance."

"That will be hard," Hayes remarked. "Look at them, they're spreading out."

"Actually that might make it easier," Barrabas said, but he was thinking about something else. "What do you think, Liam?" he asked. "If the president has panicked, he's probably sent out all of his remaining men, except his squad."

"So?"

"Would he send out his radio operator, too?"

"If he did," Nanos said, "then there's no one manning the radio. Then if fighting develops and alarms the guards inside, it might take time for them to get on the radio."

"Enough time for us to get inside," Barrabas said.

"And if we're wrong?" Hatton asked. "What if there is a man on the radio?"

All the SOBs looked at her.

"Then we'd better accomplish our task real quick," Barrabas said. "All right, listen up. Here's what we're going to do."

13

Captain Rodriguez was beside himself with rage. Being sent out into the street with eight men and having his radio operator pulled was the height of insanity!

He positioned himself on the front steps and told his men to set themselves up in twos around the house: in the front, in the back and on either side. Then he stared with feverish eyes out at the night and wondered what else it was to hold.

BILLY TWO MOVED to the back of the house. All the doubt was gone from his mind and from his soul.

It had not been a case of Hawk Spirit deserting him, but rather the spirit had tested him. Having understood that, he accepted it, and was ready to do his job the only way he knew how.

Excellently.

He moved in the darkness like a shadow, blending with it, becoming one. In his own mind he was invisible, and the two men in the back of the house could not see him.

To an observer he would have simply been a man who could move quickly and quietly. While the two soldiers were involved in a conversation, which was, of course, the main weakness of standing sentry duty in twos, Billy Two pounced on them.

His arms spread wide, he took both of them around the neck in a headlock and slammed their heads together. The smashing effect of bone against bone caused them sudden intense pain, and when he released them, they grabbed for their heads. The Osage struck both men on the jaw, one with his right fist, the other with an angled elbow, his movements sharp and powerful. The sentries staggered and then dropped to the ground, unconscious.

Next was to get access to the residence, and Billy Two went in search of a back window.

NANOS AND HAYES CIRCLED to the side of the house and saw the two guards standing together. They had stopped to light their cigarettes. Once that was accomplished, they moved away from each other.

"How do we do this?" Nanos asked.

"The hard way," Hayes said, and explained what he had in mind.

"All right," Nanos said, then leaving his M-16 with Hayes, he started walking toward the house. He had to hope that the guards didn't have a shoot-to-kill order.

He watched both men carefully and knew the exact moment when he was spotted. The sentries stiffened and raised their guns. He held his breath until he saw them closing the distance between each other, coming together to confront Nanos. That was what the SOB warriors had counted on. Safety in numbers, Hayes had said. Instinct to close ranks, and damned if he wasn't right!

One of the guards barked something at Nanos that he took to be "Halt," and he did, raising his hands.

"I give up," he said to them. "Surrender. ¿Comprendo?"

One of them pointed at him with his weapon, and he knew they wanted his gun. He took it out carefully and tossed it with an easy motion as a sentry moved to catch it. The man missed, and the gun hit the damp grass. The guard bent over and retrieved it, then he motioned for Nanos to precede them. As he did, Nanos kept up an incessant chatter, as though he were anxiously explaining something, and hoped they wouldn't hear Hayes coming up from behind.

Claude Hayes started his rush as soon as the guards had Nanos marching toward the front of the house. His knife was already drawn out when he silently approached them. Throwing his left arm around the neck of one man, he pulled him back into the blade of the knife, which punctured his right kidney. A well-directed stab to the heart finished the man off.

The other sentry was startled and took his eyes off Nanos. The Greek kicked back immediately, catching him in the stomach. He turned to face the man as he doubled over and sent another blow that landed flush on the chin. The man's head snapped back with such force that both he and Hayes heard his neck snap.

"Let's go," Nanos stated for both of them.

ON THE OTHER SIDE Liam O'Toole and Lee Hatton had managed to simultaneously remove the sentries from active duty. They had resorted to a minor diversion, setting off a small flare, and when the sentries converged on the disturbance, rushed them from the shadows. Swift and hard blows to the head relieved the sentries of further worry for a good while.

"Next step," Hatton informed O'Toole as they dragged the unconscious forms into the shadows.

BARRABAS SAW O'Toole and Hatton move toward the front of the house and assumed that Billy Two, Hayes and Nanos had also achieved their goals.

He slung his M-16 over his shoulder and began walking boldly down the street to the president's house.

BILLY TWO HAD FORCED a back window and was in the house. He closed his eyes, bringing to mind the layout of the place as it had been explained to him by Barrabas. He figured he had to be behind the stairway. He had to get up the stairway and to the radio room.

He went down the hall and then turned right, which brought him to the lobby. From there he could just get a faint whiff of cigarette smoke. Moving carefully, he inched forward along the stairway until he could see that halfway down the steps a man sat with his rifle across his knees, smoking a cigarette.

The big Osage slung his M-16 over his shoulder, backed to where he'd seen a straight-backed chair and picked it up. He set it down just behind where he figured the man's position on the stairs to be. Standing on the chair, Billy Two could reach the spindles of the wooden banister and haul himself up. He saw the man's back then and hissed at him.

The man's head jerked up. He listened intently for a few moments, then shook his head and went back to his reverie. Billy Two hissed once more. This time the guard on the stairs looked around more carefully, then crushed out the cigarette on the steps. He stood up, listening with obvious intensity, then started up the stairs.

When the man was even with him, Billy Two took all his weight on one arm and reached through the spindles with his other hand. He grabbed the man's ankle with a lightning-fast motion and pulled. The man gasped and went over backward to tumble down the stairs in a tangle of limbs.

Billy Two dropped to the floor and rushed to the front of the steps. The soldier was sprawled on his back, stunned and breathless. Billy Two brought his M-16 around and slammed the butt into the side of his head.

Satisfied that he had an unconscious opponent, he started up the stairs.

RODRIGUEZ LOOKED with disbelief at the man walking toward him and called to his men. *"¡Atención!"*

They looked at him first, then at the stranger. As the man came closer, they pointed their guns at him.

"Stop right there!" Rodriguez called out in Spanish.

"Hello, there!" the man called in English.

That encouraged Rodriguez to give his next warning in that language. "Stop! Hands up," he ordered, and for good measure motioned to his men to approach so that the intruder was between them.

"All right," the man said, holding up his hands. "Don't get nervous."

"Put your weapons down in the street."

"Okay, friend," Barrabas said, taking his M-16 off his shoulder and putting it down. "I'm not here to start any trouble."

"Your pistol."

Barrabas took out his Beretta 93-R and bent over to lay it gently on the ground, then stood, holding up his hands, palms turned outward.

"There, see? All defanged."

"What do you want?"

"I want to see President Trieste."

"Who are you?"

"What's important is that your men are being occupied by diversions, Captain. Haven't you figured that out?"

Rodriguez paused for a moment, remembering Velez telling him the same thing.

Barrabas gave Rodriguez a hard knowing look, then continued. "I'm a mercenary. I was working for the rebels until I realized their plan was doomed to failure. Of course, I had no idea you'd send all your men to their diversions," Barrabas said, scratching his head. "Maybe I should have stayed with them instead of coming over to your side."

"Coming over to my side? Why would you do that?"

"Because I want to live, friend," Barrabas said. "Now, I must see the president and tell him what I know."

"You will tell me or die." Rodriguez pointed his gun at Barrabas.

"Fine," Barrabas said. "You do that, then explain to the president that I had information to save his ass."

Rodriguez stared at Barrabas while the two eyed their captain, waiting for the command to shoot.

"Very well," Rodriguez finally said, lowering his gun and saying something to his men.

He was just holstering his gun when Barrabas moved. He dropped to the ground, sweeping one soldier's legs out from under him. As he did so, the man accidentally squeezed the trigger of his AK-47 and fired off a burst into the ground.

"Hell!" Barrabas shouted. As the first soldier toppled, Barrabas grabbed his handgun from where he had carefully placed it and slapped the other soldier across the face with it.

Both soldiers were down, but the damage was done. The burst of fire must have alerted the people in the house. Which meant, Barrabas thought, that their only hope was Billy Two.

Rodriguez turned at the sound of the gunfire and found himself looking down the barrel of a gun. There were four others trained on him by the SOBs who had closed in on him.

"Blast it, Colonel," O'Toole said to Barrabas, "you moved too fast even for us."

"Sorry," Barrabas said. "I'll try to slow it down next time."

He decided not to worry about the shots. Billy Two wasn't around, so he would simply assume that Billy was in possession of the radio room.

Fast on the heel of that thought he heard shots from inside, a quick burst, and then silence.

WHEN THEY HEARD the burst of shots from outside, the men in the president's office all rose to their feet.

From behind his desk Trieste said, "Someone get to the radio."

Velez looked at Trieste, as if to say "You idiot." To one of his men he said, "Jaime, go and check."

The man called Jaime opened the door and went out into the hall. As he started toward the radio room, a huge man appeared in the door with an AK-74.

Wait, Jaime wanted to say, wait, but he was too late. The man squeezed the trigger and Jaime leaped about the hall like a rag doll on a string.

In the office Trieste turned white and shouted, "Close the door! Close the door!"

BARRABAS LEAPED OVER to where the stunned first soldier was getting to his feet and slapped him over the head with the Beretta. After that he walked up the steps and stood in front of Captain Rodriguez to disarm the man before he got brave.

"Did you hear those shots from inside the house, Captain?" he asked. "My man has the radio room."

"You are dead men," Rodriguez stated.

"Be that as it may, Captain," Barrabas said, pressing the barrel of the Beretta to the underside of the man's chin, "I'd still like to see the president."

NANOS AND O'TOOLE STEPPED into the lobby first, guns held ready. Behind them Captain Rodriguez was pushed into the lobby, followed closely by Barrabas. Taking up the rear were Hayes and Hatton.

Lying at the base of the stairs was a soldier, his arms spread out at his sides. There was blood oozing from the side of his head, but he was alive.

"How many more men in the house, Captain?" Barrabas asked.

"None," the captain said. "The house is empty except for the president."

Barrabas poked the captain hard in the small of the back with the Beretta. "You expect us to believe that you left your president here alone?"

"He demanded it. He wanted all his men out in the street."

"What is your name, Captain?"

"Rodriguez."

"Captain Rodriguez, you are a very poor liar," Barrabas said, again poking the captain with the gun in the same spot. If the man lived, he would have a dandy bruise there to show for it.

"Let's go upstairs," Barrabas said, pushing the man forward, "you first. If anyone up there is trigger-happy, you'll be the first to know it."

Rodriguez proceeded reluctantly until they reached the base of the steps then said, "Wait, wait!"

"Getting smart?" Barrabas asked. "We know about the special squad. All we want to know is if there are any other soldiers in the house besides them. That's not such a hard question. They're a real special squad, getting better treatment than you and your men, so what do you owe them?"

Rodriguez thought that over and saw the truth in it. Why should he die for Velez, the thought came to him with sudden force.

"How many other men?" Barrabas asked.

"None," Rodriguez finally said. "There is only the president and his special squad." He'd said "special squad" as if it were two four-letter words.

"Ah," Barrabas said, and gave the man a sharp but controlled blow to the head. "Thank you, Captain, and this will make sure you continue to cooperate."

THINGS WERE TENSE in the president's office.

"I want you all here!"

"Presidente," Velez answered, "there is nothing we can do here. We must go face the enemy."

"You sent a man out there, and you saw what happened!"

You sent him out there to his death, not me, Velez corrected silently.

Trieste looked around the room with the jerky head motions of a rat trapped in a corner. It occurred to him in his panic that if only he had put in connecting doors to this room the way he wanted to, there would be another exit.

"We'll wait for them," Trieste said. "Maybe the others will return before they get to us."

Velez looked at his president, wondered why he was loyal to such a man, and realized he was loyal to his country and the dignity of the office.

"As you wish, *presidente*."

"ARE WE GOING UP, Colonel?" Nanos asked.

"Judging from the condition of this joker," O'Toole said, indicating the fallen soldier, "Billy Two must already be up there."

"Fan out," Barrabas ordered. "We'll check the downstairs first."

"Yes, sir," O'Toole replied.

He and Hayes moved left while Nanos and Hatton moved right. Barrabas went straight back, behind the stairs, and found the window that Billy Two must have forced to get in.

He returned to the lobby and waited for the others to come back.

"Nothing," Hayes and O'Toole reported. Seconds later Hatton and Nanos returned and repeated the same.

"Okay," Barrabas said, "let's go up for the finale."

BILLY TWO STOOD in the doorway of the radio room, waiting for someone else to poke his head out of the room down the hall, past the stairs. Briefly he had considered riddling the radio with bullets, but decided that they might end up needing it. So he simply stood guard over the room, because that was his part of this particular operation. He was curious about the shots he'd heard outside, but he couldn't allow his curiosity to affect his course of action. He had to stay put, even if those shots meant that the other SOBs had been taken.

He'd know what was going on very soon, depending on who came up those steps in the next five seconds.

THE SOBs TOOK to the stairs in a staggered line. O'Toole went up first on the right, followed by Nanos on the left and Barrabas in the center. After that Hatton started up on the right side and Hayes on the left. If something went wrong, it would take more than one burst from an AK-47 to take them all out.

When O'Toole reached the top, he could look to the right, away from the radio room, without craning his neck much, but not to the left. That would mean sticking his neck out—something he had never been fond of doing.

Nanos came up on the right side of the steps, and he was able to look to the left. He saw an empty hall, but couldn't see more without exposing himself.

O'Toole and Nanos looked at each other, nodded and then each checked out his area of visibility, covering each other at the same time.

"Don't move!" Nanos said to O'Toole. The Irishman froze. Very slowly Nanos said, "Billy Two has his gun pointed right at your head."

O'Toole frowned, then said to Nanos, "You silly son of a bitch!"

"Straight ahead," Barrabas growled right behind them.

14

O'Toole and Nanos moved up into the hall and flattened themselves against the wall. Barrabas came up next and moved toward the radio room. Hatton and Hayes remained on the stairs, just at the top.

"What's happening?" Barrabas asked Billy Two.

"Door down the hall opened and a soldier stepped out. That's him lying in the hall."

"What door?"

"From the description we got, it's the door to the president's office."

"Any more in there?"

"I heard several different voices."

"Pin it down."

Billy Two thought a moment, then said, "Five, six."

"His squad," Barrabas said. "Stay by the radio, Billy. Try and find their frequency. If they're coming back, they should first report back."

It struck Barrabas that it would have been a good idea to bring a Salvadoran with them to sit on the radio. If they had, they might have redirected any troops who were going to come back early. Now they'd just have to hope that they had time to pry the president out from hiding.

Barrabas moved back out into the hallway.

"We'll have to get him out of his office," he told the others.

"Is the squad in there with him?" O'Toole asked.

"That's what Billy figures," Barrabas said.

"Any other ways in or out?" O'Toole asked.

"Not according to Berbick," Barrabas said. "Judging by the exterior, there are no other ways out of the building from there."

"What about connecting doors to the rooms next to it?" Nanos asked.

"That's what we're going to find out," Barrabas said.

CAPTAIN VELEZ HAD his ear glued to the door and fleetingly considered how ridiculous he must look. His men were gathered around him—all but Barrio, who stood by the president's desk.

"What do you hear?" Trieste asked. His eyes had a wild look in them, and he was clutching a Makarov pistol tightly in his hand.

"I heard voices," Velez said. He turned to face the president. "If we open the door now and move quickly, we might be able to surprise them."

"No!" Trieste shouted. "We will wait for them. They have to come through that door, and when they do, we shall be ready."

Velez had to admit one thing. As much as he disliked being cooped up in the office, the rebels did have to come through the door, which gave him and his people an edge.

"Yes, sir," Velez said, and pressed his ear to the door again.

IN LOW TONES Barrabas gave the SOBs their instructions. Based on the thickness of the walls in the hall, Barrabas had worked out a plan he thought would work. He decided to pull Billy Two from the radio room. He wouldn't understand the transmissions, anyway.

They moved down the hall in twos: O'Toole and Nanos to the left, Hatton and Hayes to the right, and Barrabas and Billy Two down the center, with Billy directly behind Barrabas.

Nanos and O'Toole stopped by the door to the room on the left of the president's office. Barrabas and Billy Two flattened themselves against the wall on either side of the office door. Hatton and Hayes continued on and stopped by a door just beyond the office.

At a gesture from Barrabas both of the other teams opened their doors and stepped inside quickly. Barrabas waited for a signal from them. After a few moments Nanos appeared at one door and Hatton at the other. Both shook their heads to show that there were no connecting doors. Barrabas indicated they should go ahead with the plan they'd discussed for the eventuality. He looked at his watch and held up two fingers to both of them.

"Two minutes," he mouthed to Billy Two, who nodded.

"WE'RE GOING TO DIE," Roberto Barrio said.

"What? What?" Trieste said.

Velez turned and looked at Barrio. "What are you saying?"

"We're trapped, and if we stay here with him we'll die," Barrio said.

"He is our president, Barrio," Velez said. "It is our duty to die if we must to protect him."

"To protect *him*?" Barrio asked, pointing at the sweating, panicky Trieste.

"It does not matter what he is," Velez said, "he is *el presidente*."

But Barrio wasn't listening. He had already calculated the odds for his own survival, which was the only meaningful thing for him. Then he did what no other man in the room would have dreamed of doing.

He raised his Makarov pistol and shot President Caesar Armande Trieste in the head.

AT THE SOUND of the report from inside the room Barrabas shouted, "Go, go, go!"

On the left side Liam O'Toole pointed his M-16 at the wall and fired. He outlined the door with a zing of hot bullets, and on the right side Claude Hayes did the same thing.

In the hall Billy Two prepared to kick in the door.

THE MAN SAGGED in the chair, his head lolling to one side.

Velez and the others stared at Barrio in shock, but before anybody could cry out "What have you done!" gunfire began to punch the walls.

The wall on both sides of the room suddenly seemed to sprout doorways—5.56-caliber doorways. Velez wasn't quite sure which way to turn, and his men were even more confused than he was, looking to him for guidance.

Suddenly the firing stopped and outlined portions of the wall were kicked inward.

"Fire! Fire!" Velez shouted, and began firing through one of the walls.

Billy Two and Barrabas rushed into the room, their M-16s on automatic, and sprayed the room with deadly fire. Velez and his men found death slamming into them. The other SOBs rushed through their makeshift doors and began firing in controlled bursts. With the appearance of the others, Barrabas and Billy Two also modified their firing. None of them could haphazardly spray the room without injuring one another, but there was no need for that anymore.

They all stopped to slam new magazines home before they walked around the room, checking the damage.

"They're all dead, Colonel," O'Toole said.

"Even the president?"

"He was dead before we got into the room."

"That shot we heard?" Barrabas said.

O'Toole examined the body and noted the hole in the left temple. "One of his men apparently decided he didn't like his president anymore. Still, we couldn't have known. And from the looks of things, the others stayed loyal. We did the right thing, no question about it."

"Where's the radio?" Barrabas asked.

"I've got it," Hatton said, handing it over.

"Berbick, do you read me?" He waited a moment, then repeated, "Berbick, do you read me?"

"Damn—" a voice said in annoyance through a crackle of static, then, "Yes, this is Berbick."

"Come and get it," Barrabas told him. "Now!"

Barrabas turned to O'Toole and said, "The new owner is coming."

Barrabas then sent Billy Two and Nanos downstairs to look after the wounded soldiers and to watch for Berbick.

"I hope," O'Toole said, as the other two left the room, "Berbick will get here before the soldiers."

"Yes, but when he does," Hatton asked, "will they accept him?"

"That's the way it is in Central America, Lee," O'Toole said. "They're loyal to whoever has the power."

"And if Berbick can get here in time," Barrabas said, "he'll have it."

"Maybe he'll steal a jeep," Hatton said.

"Colonel!" Nanos called from downstairs.

Barrabas left the office and along with Hatton, Hayes and O'Toole went to join Nanos. The two wounded soldiers had been removed from the lobby.

"The new president is here," the Greek said and pointed toward the open front entrance.

Berbick was getting out of a jeep that had been driven by Francisco.

"You have done it!" Francisco said.

"Liam, take President Berbick upstairs," Barrabas said.

"Francisco will accompany me," Berbick announced. "He is to be the captain of my guard."

"Congratulations," Barrabas said, then as the beaming man went by him, Barrabas grabbed his arm and said, "Uh, Francisco, where did you get the jeep?"

"While our people kept the soldiers running in circles," he said happily, "I stole it."

Francisco went inside in the wake of Berbick, and Hatton looked at Barrabas and smiled.

At that moment several more jeeps pulled into the main street, followed by soldiers on foot.

"There's a lot of 'em," Hayes acknowledged.

"And they're not ours." Barrabas looked at Hayes and said, "Get Berbick back out here fast. Now we find out if he can save our butts or not."

But half an hour later nobody had any doubts left as Jules reentered the house, leaving behind him the sound of resounding cheers.

"My people have accepted me," he announced to Barrabas.

"Glad to hear it," Barrabas said. "That means our job is done."

"Will you stay with us awhile?" Berbick asked. "As my guests, of course."

"We appreciate the offer, Mr. President," Barrabas said, "but we've got a boat to catch."

"If it's still there," Nanos added under his breath.

"LUCKILY," Nile Barrabas said to Walker Jessup ten days later in Kingston, Jamaica, "the boat was still there. Of course, the outboard had drifted away, so we ended up swimming out to it."

"Sounds like a fitting end to an interesting mission," Jessup said.

They were at the Kingston Hyatt Regency, sitting out by the pool. Jessup had arrived only that morning, and it was the first chance they'd had to talk about the mission.

"Where are the others?"

"All the ones who've been on the mission are on their way," Barrabas said. "So the monies are all deposited in the accounts?" Barrabas asked in confirmation.

Jessup suddenly found the liquid in his glass extremely interesting.

"Jessup?" Barrabas said, leaning forward, "it's all settled, isn't it?"

"You did a good job, Nile," Jessup said. "I, uh, did tell you that this was sort of a shoestring operation, didn't I?"

"I believe you did mention something about that," Barrabas said in an ominously quiet tone. "But that I understood to refer to the resources available for this particular job. But the usual fee is what I expect otherwise. And will get—" he paused to give the Fixer a hard look "—one way or another."

Jessup scratched his nose and said, "Yes, you will, Nile."

"When?"

"Soon."

"How soon?"

"How about this afternoon?" Jessup said at last.

Barrabas sat back in his patio chair and said, "Thank your lucky stars or I would have sold you for shark bait. Now how about lunch? I need to fortify myself for one more task, the most difficult one yet." He lifted his glass and with an inscrutable look added, "Here's to your health, fat man."

EPILOGUE

The woman trod softly on the jungle trail, her steps measured, deliberate, even though she was distracted. Clearly, her face was troubled, and if the moisture in her eyes did not reveal her distress, then her furrowed brow certainly did. She was looking for someone, but the search was not the reason for her anxiety. The man she sought had to be close by, as her instincts and knowledge of his habits over many years told her he would be.

Suddenly a twig snapped underfoot and in the quiet tropical night it sounded like a pistol shot. Ten feet ahead the tall figure with the shock of white hair whirled and drew his sidearm in one fluid motion, the snout of his weapon an extension of himself, probing the moonlit scene.

"Nile, I . . ." Lee Hatton began.

"Come, I was wondering when you'd show," Nile Barrabas replied, his voice coaxing. He holstered the weapon.

"Sorry I disturbed you," Lee Hatton continued, "but what I need to know cannot wait."

"Save your sorrow for what's important, Lee."

She climbed the slight rise to where Barrabas stood, and placed her arms around him. He, in turn, made the same gesture, but the embrace was one of brotherly affection.

"Is it...true?" There was a slight catch in her voice as if the question demanded extra effort.

"Yes, Lee, Geoff is dead."

Lee Hatton stiffened perceptibly at Barrabas's words, then she took one pace backward to look him in the face.

"Isn't it ironic, I mean, I could be considered some sort of healer, a reliever of pain. But what I feel inside..." Her voice trailed off and she turned away from Barrabas, but not quickly enough for him to miss the single tear coursing down one cheek.

"Lee, this business that we involve ourselves in means that we present our lives at every heartbeat. We're fortunate each time we walk away physically unscathed, doubly so when we escape emotional anguish, if one of the others should fall."

Barrabas stepped forward and touched her shoulder gently, making her face him.

"There's nothing more I can say except it's perhaps the reason that Nate has made the decision to remain on call rather than accompany us on every mission."

Lee Hatton wondered if this was Barrabas's way of sparing her, softening the blow of Geoff Bishop's death by springing this sudden and surprising new information. She decided not; it wasn't like Nile.

"Thank you for the support. But I don't think anything can help this sense of emptiness." She tried for a smile and failed. Barrabas waited for her to continue. "And I didn't want to let you see me cry. After all, I'm supposed to be the battle-hardened warrior, right?"

"No thanks needed, Lee. And I would have been surprised if you had felt any other way. But if it's any consolation, let me say this, time will take the edge off the pain.''

Lee Hatton turned away with a sigh, nodded and walked into the darkness.

Take
4 explosive books
plus a
mystery bonus
FREE

TAKE 'EM NOW

FOLDING SUNGLASSES
FROM GOLD EAGLE

Mean up your act with these tough, street-smart shades. Practical, too, because they fold 3 times into a handy, zip-up polyurethane pouch that fits neatly into your pocket. Rugged metal frame. Scratch-resistant acrylic lenses. Best of all, they can be yours for only $6.99.

MAIL YOUR ORDER TODAY.

Send your name, address, and zip code, along with a check or money order for just $6.99 + .75¢ for postage and handling (for a total of $7.74) payable to Gold Eagle Reader Service. (New York and Iowa residents please add applicable sales tax.)

Remove from pouch...

unfold once...

GOLD EAGLE

Gold Eagle Reader Service
901 Fuhrmann Blvd.
P.O. Box 1396
Buffalo, N.Y. 14240-1396

unfold twice...

and they're ready to wear.

GES-1A

Offer not available in Canada.